ALSO BY SARAH ADDISON ALLEN

The Girl Who Chased the Moon

The Sugar Queen

Garden Spells

The

PEACH KEEPER

The

PEACH KEEPER

A NOVEL

Sarah Addison Allen

BANTAM BOOKS

NEW YORK

Copyright © 2011 by Sarah Addison Allen

Published in the United States by Bantam Books, an imprint of The Random House Publishing Group, a division of Random House, Inc., New York.

BANTAM BOOKS and the rooster colophon are registered trademarks of Random House, Inc.

ISBN 978-1-61793-270-0

Printed in the United States of America

Book design by Mary A. Wirth

To Michelle Pittman and Heidi Gibbs.

Everything I know of friendship

is thanks to you.

The
PEACH KEEPER

Hiding Places

The day Paxton Osgood took the box of heavy-stock, foil-lined envelopes to the post office, the ones she'd had a professional calligrapher address, it began to rain so hard the air turned as white as bleached cotton. By nightfall, rivers had crested at flood stage and, for the first time since 1936, the mail couldn't be delivered. When things began to dry out, when basements were pumped free of water and branches were cleared from yards and streets, the invitations were finally delivered, but to all the wrong houses. Neighbors laughed over fences, handing the misdelivered pieces of mail to their rightful owners with comments about the crazy weather and their careless postman. The next day, an unusual number of people showed up at the doctor's office with infected paper cuts, because the envelopes had sealed, cementlike, from the moisture. Later, the single-card invitations themselves seemed to hide and pop back up at random. Mrs. Jameson's invitation disappeared for two days, then reappeared in a bird's nest outside. Harper Rowley's invitation was found in the church bell tower, Mr. Kingsley's in his elderly mother's garden shed.

If anyone had been paying attention to the signs, they would have realized that air turns white when things are about to change, that paper cuts mean there's more to what's written on the page than meets the eye, and that birds are always out to protect you from things you don't see.

But no one was paying attention. Least of all Willa Jackson.

The envelope sat untouched on the back counter of Willa's store for over a week. She picked it up curiously when it had been delivered with the other mail, but then she'd dropped it like it had burned her as soon as she'd recognized what it was. Even now, when she walked by it, she would throw a suspicious glance its way.

"Open it already," Rachel finally said with exasperation that morning. Willa turned to Rachel Edney, who was standing behind the coffee bar across the store. She had short dark hair and, in her capris and sport tank, looked like she was ready to go climb a large rock. No matter how many times Willa told her she didn't actually have to dress in the clothes the store sold—Willa herself rarely deviated from jeans and boots—Rachel was convinced she had to represent.

"I'm not going. No need to open it," Willa said, deciding to take on the mundane task of folding the new stock of organic T-shirts, hoping it would help her ignore the strange feeling that came over her every time she thought of that invitation, like a balloon of expectation expanding in the center of her body. She used to feel this way a lot when she was younger, right before she did something really stupid. But she thought she was past all of that. She'd padded her life with so much calm that she didn't think anything could penetrate it. Some things, apparently, still could.

Rachel made a tsking sound. "You're such an elitist."

That made Willa laugh. "Explain to me why not opening an invitation to a gala thrown by the richest women in town makes *me* elitist."

"You look at everything they do with disdain, like they're just too silly to be believed."

"I do *not*."

"Well, it's either that or you're repressing a secret desire to be one of them," Rachel said as she put on a green apron with *Au Naturel Sporting Goods and Café* embroidered on it in yellow script.

Rachel was eight years younger than Willa, but Willa had never written off Rachel's opinions as those of just another twenty-two-year-old who thought she knew everything. Rachel had lived a vagabond and bohemian life, and she knew a lot about human nature. The only reason she had settled in Walls of Water, for now, was because she'd fallen in love with a man here. Love, she always said, changes the game.

But Willa didn't want to get into what she did or didn't feel about the rich families in town. Rachel had never spent more than a few months in any one place growing up. Willa had lived here almost her whole life. She inherently understood the mysterious social dynamics of Walls of Water; she just didn't know how to explain them to people who didn't. So Willa asked the one question she knew would distract Rachel. "What's on the menu today? It smells fantastic."

"Ah. Excellent stuff, if I do say so myself. Trail mix with chocolate-covered coffee beans, oatmeal cookies with coffee icing, and espresso brownies." She gestured like a game-show hostess to the snacks in the glass case under the counter.

Almost a year ago, Willa had let Rachel take over the previously closed coffee bar in the store and gave her the go-ahead to put snacks that had coffee as an ingredient on the menu. It had turned out to be a great idea. Walking into the shop in the mornings was actually a pleasure now. Being met by the sharp scent of chocolate mingling with the moist scent of brewing coffee had a dark, secretive feel to it, like Willa had finally found the perfect place to hide.

Willa's store, which specialized in organic sportswear, was on National Street, the main road leading to the entrance of Cataract National Forest, widely known for its beautiful waterfalls, in the heart of North Carolina's Blue Ridge Mountains. All the shops catering to the hikers and campers were located here, in one long, busy stretch. And it was here that Willa had finally found her niche, if it could be called that. Truthfully, she didn't care much for hiking or camping or any of the outdoorsy stuff that sustained the town, but she was so much more comfortable with the other shop owners and the people new to town than she was with the people she knew in her youth. If she had to be here, this was where she belonged, not with the glittery townies.

The stores were housed in old buildings that had been built more than a century ago, when Walls of Water was just a tiny logging town. The ceilings were pierced tin, and the floors were nail-worn and lemony. With the slightest pressure, they creaked and popped like an old woman's bones, which was how Willa knew Rachel had approached her.

She turned and saw Rachel extending the dreaded envelope. "Open it."

Willa reluctantly took it. It was thick and rich, and felt like cashmere paper. Just to get Rachel off her back, she tore it open. The moment she did, the bell above the door rang, and they both looked up to see who it was.

But no one was there.

Rachel rubbed her bare arms, which were goose-pimply. "I just got a chill."

"My grandmother would say that meant a ghost passed by you."

Rachel snorted. "Superstitions are man's way of trying to control things he has no control over."

"Thank you, Margaret Mead."

"Go on." Rachel nudged her. "Read it."

Willa took out the invitation and read:

On August 12, 1936, a small group of ladies in Walls of Water, North Carolina, formed a society that has since become the most important social club in the area, one that organizes fundraisers, sponsors local cultural events, and gives out yearly scholarships.

It is with great pride that the current members of the Women's Society Club invite you, as a past member or relative of a past member, to a special commemoration of the 75th anniversary of the formation of this great organization.

Come help us celebrate 75 years of sparkling good deeds. The party will be the first event held in the newly restored Blue Ridge Madam, on August 12 at 7 p.m.

RSVP with the enclosed card to Paxton Osgood, President.

"See?" Rachel said from over Willa's shoulder. "That's not so bad."

"I can't believe Paxton's holding it in the Blue Ridge Madam."

"Oh, come on. I'd give anything to see the inside of that place, and so would you."

"I'm not going."

"You're crazy to pass this up. Your grandmother—"

"Helped found the club, I know," Willa finished for her as she set the invitation aside. "She did, I didn't."

"It's your legacy."

"It has nothing to do with me."

Rachel threw her hands in the air. "I give up. Do you want some coffee?"

"Yes," Willa said, glad for the end of this conversation. "Soy milk and two sugars." Just this past week, Rachel had become convinced that how people took their coffee gave some secret insight into their characters. Were people who took their coffee black unyielding? Did people who liked their coffee with milk and no sugar have mother issues? She had a notebook behind the coffee counter in which she wrote her findings. Willa decided to keep her on her toes by making up a different request every day.

Rachel walked back to the coffee bar to write that down in her notebook. "Hmm, interesting," she said seriously, as if it made all the sense in the world, as if she'd finally figured Willa out.

"You don't believe in ghosts, but you do believe that how I take my coffee says something about my personality."

"That's superstition. This is *science*."

Willa shook her head and went back to folding shirts, trying to ignore the invitation, now sitting on the table. But it kept catching her eye, fluttering slightly, as if caught in a breeze.

She flopped a shirt over it and tried to forget about it.

When they closed up shop that evening, Rachel headed off to meet her boyfriend for an evening hike, which was so annoyingly healthy that Willa made up for it by taking a brownie out of the snack case and eating it in three big bites. Then she got in her bright yellow Jeep Wrangler to go home to do laundry. Wednesday nights were always laundry nights. Sometimes she even looked forward to it.

Her life was monotonous, but it kept her out of trouble. She was thirty years old. This, her father would say, was called being an adult.

But instead of heading straight home, Willa turned onto Jackson Hill, her private daily detour. It was a steep mountain slope and a dramatic drive, almost foreboding, but it was the only way to get to the antebellum mansion at the top, locally known as the Blue Ridge Madam. Ever since renovation had started on the place well over a year ago, Willa had made these secret treks up the hill to watch the progress.

The place had been abandoned years ago by the last in a series of shady developers. It had fallen into disrepair and had been slowly disintegrating when the Osgood family stepped in and bought it. Now almost fully restored, and soon to be a bed-and-breakfast with a banquet hall, the wide white Doric columns were back, spanning the length of the house in a dramatic neoclassic fashion. The lower portico now had a period-piece chandelier hanging from the ceiling. The upper portico had cast-iron chairs on it. And it was now a startling mass of windows, whereas before they'd all been broken and boarded up. It looked like something out of the old South, a plantation manor where women in hoop skirts fanned themselves and men in suits talked about crop prices.

The Madam had been built in the 1800s by Willa's great-great-grandfather, the founder of the now-defunct Jackson Logging Company. It had been a wedding gift to his young wife—a beautiful, delicate woman from a prominent family in Atlanta. She'd loved the house, considered it her equal, but she had hated this mountain town called Walls of Water, hated its lonely green wetness. She'd been known for throwing elaborate balls in hopes of coaxing the citizens to become as fine as she wanted them to be. It never happened. Not able to make society out of what she had, she'd decided to bring society to her instead. She'd persuaded her friends from Atlanta to come for visits, to build homes, to treat this place as a playful paradise, something she'd never felt herself, but she'd been very good at convincing others. It was the particular magic of beautiful, unsatisfied women.

And so a rich society had formed in this tiny North Carolina town surrounded by waterfalls, a town once populated mainly by rough logging men. These well-to-do families were curious, incongruous, and stubborn. Not welcome at all. But when the government bought the surrounding mountain forest and turned it into a national park, and the local logging industry dried up, it was these families who helped the town survive.

The irony was that the Jacksons, once the finest family in town, the reason for the town's existence in the first place, lost all their money when the logging stopped. The memory of who they used to be, and the money they used to have, sustained them for a while. But then they couldn't pay their taxes and had been forced to move out of the Madam. Most who had the last name of Jackson left town. But one stayed, a teenager named Georgie Jackson—Willa's grand-mother. She was seventeen, unmarried, and pregnant. She became, of all things, a maid to the Osgood family, who were once great friends to the Jacksons.

Willa pulled to the side of the road just before the turn to the driveway up to the Madam. She always timed it so that she got here after the crew had left for the day. She got out of her Wrangler and climbed onto the hood, leaning back against the windshield. It was late July, the hottest, thickest part of summer, alive with the drone of lovesick insects. She put on her sunglasses against the setting sun and stared up at the house.

The only thing left to the renovation was the land-scaping, which apparently had gotten under way just that day. That excited Willa. New things to study. She could see that there were wooden stakes and string markers making a patchwork of squares across the front yard, and there were different-colored dashes painted on the grass, indicating where the under-ground utility lines were so workers wouldn't dig there. Most of the activity, however, seemed centered on the area around the only tree on the flat top of the hill, where the house sat.

The tree was right at the precipice of the left slope. Its leaves grew in long, thin bunches, and its limbs were stretched wide. When light hit the tree at just the

right time in the evening, it actually looked like someone on the edge of a cliff, about to dive into the ocean.
A backhoe was parked next to the tree, and plastic
strings were tied around the branches.

They were going to take it down?

She wondered why. It seemed perfectly healthy.

Well, whatever they did, it was guaranteed to be for
the better. The Osgoods were known for their good
taste. The Blue Ridge Madam was going to be a show-
place again.

As much as Willa didn't want to admit it, Rachel was
right. She would love to see what the inside looked like.
She just didn't think she had any right to. The house
hadn't been in her family since the 1930s. Even getting
this close felt like trespassing . . . which, if she was
honest with herself, was one of the reasons she did it.
But she'd never even had the nerve to get close enough
to look in when she was a teenager, and it had been a
right of passage to break into the decaying house. In
her youth, she'd pulled every prank known to man, and
had been so good at it that no one had known it was her
until the very end. She'd been a legend her graduating
class had called the Walls of Water High School Joker.
But this place was different. It'd had a mysterious
push-pull effect on her, and still did. Every teenager
who had ever broken into the house had come away
with stories of mysterious footsteps and slamming
doors and a dark fedora that floated through the air, as
if worn by an invisible man. Maybe that was what had
always kept her from getting too close. Ghosts scared
her, thanks to her grandmother.

Willa sat up and reached into the back pocket of her jeans. She brought out the invitation and read it again. It said to RSVP with the enclosed card, so Willa looked in the envelope for the card and brought it out.

She was surprised to find a Post-it attached to it that read:

Willa:
Your grandmother and my grandmother are the only two surviving members of the original club, and I'd like to plan something special for them at the party. Call me and let's try to work something out.
Pax

Her handwriting was pretty, of course. Willa remembered that from high school. She had once taken a note that Paxton had accidentally dropped in the hallway and kept it for months—a strange list about characteristics Paxton wanted her future husband to have. She'd read it over and over, studying Paxton's sloping y's and jaunty x's. She'd studied it so much, she found she could replicate it. And once she'd had that skill, it had been impossible not to use it, which had resulted in a very embarrassing encounter between uppity Paxton Osgood and Robbie Roberts, the school's own redneck lothario, who'd thought Paxton had sent him a love letter.

The Walls of Water High School Joker had struck again.

"Beautiful, isn't it?"

Willa jumped at the voice, her heart giving a sudden

kick in her chest. She dropped the invitation, and it flew on the wind to the owner of the voice, standing a few feet to the right of her Wrangler.

He had on dark trousers with a blue paisley tie sticking out of one of his pockets. His white dress shirt was translucent with sweat, and his dark hair was sticking to his forehead and neck. Mirrored sunglasses hid his eyes. The invitation hit him flat against his chest and flapped there like a fish out of water. He smiled slightly, tiredly, as he peeled it off, as if this was the last thing he wanted to deal with right now. This was a sign, she thought. Though of what, she had no idea. It was just what her grandmother would say when something unexpected happened, usually accompanied by instructions to knock three times and turn in a circle, or put chestnuts and pennies on the windowsill.

He took off his sunglasses and looked up at her. A strange expression came over his face, and he said, "It's *you*."

She stared at him until she understood. *Oh, God*. To be caught here was one thing; to be caught here by one of them was something else entirely. Mortified, Willa quickly slid off the hood and darted inside the Jeep. It was a sign, all right. A sign that meant *Run away as fast as you can*.

"Wait," she heard him say as she started the engine.

But she didn't wait. She kicked the Jeep in gear and raced away.

TWO

Whispers

Paxton Osgood had stayed late to finish some paper-work at the outreach center, so it was dusk when she left. She drove home, following the flickering lights of lampposts as they popped on, like drowsy fireflies leading her way. She parked in front of her parents' house and got out of her car thinking that, if she timed this right, she would be able to have a quick swim before changing and heading back out to the Women's Society Club meeting that evening.

This plan was carefully hinged on not facing her parents. She'd spent weeks tinkering with her schedule just so she wouldn't have to stop and tell them about her day the moment she came in. This impatience, this avoidance, was a fairly new development, and she wasn't sure what to do about it. Up until now, she'd never really minded living with her parents. Once a season, when she went to visit her Tulane sorority sisters in New Orleans, they would all marvel that Paxton still lived at home. They didn't understand why she'd gone back to live with her parents after graduation in the first place, when she had the money to do whatever she wanted. It was hard to explain. She loved Walls of Water. She loved being a part of its history, of keeping it going. It struck a deep, resonant chord in her. She *belonged* here. And since Paxton's twin brother Colin's job took him all over the country, and sometimes overseas, Paxton felt it was only fair that their parents have at least one child nearby.

But last year, as age thirty loomed ahead of her like a black balloon, Paxton had finally made the decision to move out, not to another state, not even across town, but to a townhouse that her friend and realtor Kirsty Lemon was trying to sell, a mere 6.3 miles from Hickory Cottage. She'd measured it on her car's odometer and offered it up as a major selling point to her parents. But her mother had been so upset at the thought of her leaving, of breaking up their happy little dysfunctional unit, that she'd been forced to back out. She did, however, move out of the main house and into the pool house, a small step but a necessary one. This was just going to take time.

The pool house gave her some privacy, but unfortunately there was no way to get to it without walking through the main house, so her parents always knew when she was coming and going. She couldn't even bring in bags of groceries without her mother's commentary. This was what her daydreams had come to. She fantasized about keeping a box of doughnuts on her kitchen counter and having no one comment on them.

She walked up the steps to her parents' sprawling home, called Hickory Cottage because of the large number of hickory trees on the estate. In the autumn, the entire backyard became a mass of lollipop-yellow leaves, so bright they lit up the night like daylight. Birds nesting in the trees would get confused because they couldn't tell what time of day it was, and they would stay awake for days until they dropped out of the branches with exhaustion.

She opened the front door silently, then clicked it shut behind her, knowing her parents would be watching CNN in the den. She would just tiptoe to the kitchen and out the French doors without them ever knowing.

She turned, and promptly fell over a suitcase.

She landed on her hands on the marble floor of the foyer, her palms stinging.

"What on earth was that?" Paxton heard her mother say. Then there was a rush of footsteps coming from the den.

Paxton sat up and saw that the contents of her tote bag had spilled out during her fall. All her lists were scattered around, which instantly made her panic. Her lists were private. She never let anyone see them. She quickly picked them up and stuffed them back into her bag, just as three people appeared in the foyer.

"Paxton! Are you all right?" her mother asked as Paxton stood and brushed herself off. "Colin, do some-thing about these suitcases, for heaven's sake."

"I was going to take them to the pool house, but that was before I discovered Paxton had moved out there," Colin said.

At the sound of her brother's voice, Paxton spun to face him. She instantly ran into his arms. "You weren't supposed to be here until Friday!" she said, squeezing him tightly, her eyes closed, breathing in that calm, easygoing air he always carried around him. She thought she might cry, she was so happy to see him. Then she was so mad she thought about hitting him. Dealing with her parents would be so much easier if he would just stop wandering around and come home for good.

"Things wrapped up sooner than I thought on my last project," he said, pulling back and looking at her. "You look great, Pax. Move out and get married al-ready."

"No, don't tell her to get married!" their mother, Sophia, said. "Do you know who she's seeing right now? Sebastian Rogers."

"I'm not seeing him, Mama. We're just friends."

"Sebastian Rogers," Colin repeated as he looked at Paxton. "Didn't we go to school with him? The effemi-nate kid in the purple trench coat?"

"Yes, that's him," their mother said, as if Colin had agreed with her about something.

Paxton felt her jaw tighten. "He doesn't wear a pur-ple trench coat anymore. He's a dentist."

Colin hesitated a few beats before changing the

subject. "I guess I'll put my suitcases in the guest suite upstairs, then."

"Nonsense. You'll put them in your old room. Everything's just the way you left it," Sophia said, then she grabbed her husband's arm. "Donald, our babies are both here! Isn't this wonderful? Get some champagne."

He turned with a nod and left the foyer.

Over the years, Paxton's father had slowly let his wife take over everything, to the point that now he mutely left all decisions up to her, and most of his time was spent at the golf course. As much as Paxton understood her mother's drive, and how much easier it was to do things yourself than to let others do them, she often wondered why her mother didn't resent her husband's absence. Wasn't that the whole point to being married? That you had a partner, someone you trusted, to help with important decisions?

"I can only stay for one drink," Paxton said. "I'm sorry, Colin. I have a club meeting."

He shook his head. "Don't worry. We'll catch up later. I need to go out for a while this evening, too."

Sophia reached over and brushed some of the unruly hair off her son's forehead. "Your first night here, and you're going out?"

Colin grinned at her. "And you can no longer give me a curfew. Drives you crazy, doesn't it?"

"Oh, you," she said as she walked toward the kitchen, motioning for them to follow her with a flick of her perfectly manicured hand. Her tennis bracelet caught the light and sparkled, as if she were trying to hypnotize them into doing her bidding.

As soon as she was out of earshot, Paxton sighed and said, "Thank God you're here. Will you please *move back already?*"

"I'm not through sowing my wild oats." He shrugged his lanky shoulders. All her family was tall but, at six-five, Colin was by far the tallest. In high school, his friends used to call him Stick Man. His hair was darker than hers—which was a blond she kept meticulously highlighted—but they shared the same dark Osgood eyes.

"You still wear a suit to work," she pointed out. "That's not wild oats."

He shrugged again.

"Are you okay?" she asked.

"I've been up for two days straight. I need sleep. So what's up with you and this Sebastian character?"

Paxton looked away and adjusted her tote bag on her shoulder. "We're just friends. Mama doesn't approve."

"Does she ever? The Blue Ridge Madam looks fantastic, by the way. Better even than the photos you emailed me. I went up there late this afternoon. There are a few landscaping changes I need to make now that I've seen it in person, but otherwise it looks like everything is on track."

"Are you sure it will be done before the gala next month?"

He reached out and squeezed her hand, and it almost made her cry again. "I promise."

"Champagne!" their father called as he stomped up the basement steps. Colin and Paxton sighed in unison, then went to join their parents.

That night's Women's Society Club meeting was being held at Kirsty Lemon's house, Lemon Tree Cottage. When Paxton got there that evening, Lemon Tree was decked out in all things lemon. The paper lanterns following the walkway to the front of the house had die-cut images of lemon wedges. The topiaries at the door had fake lemons on them. The door itself was covered in shiny yellow paper. Somehow, over the years, these meetings had become less about the actual charities they supported and more about trying to outdo one another in presentation.

Paxton went to the door and knocked. After drinks with her family, she had changed from her work clothes into a white dress and heels, then left at the same time as her brother. Their parents had actually waved to them from the driveway.

Kirsty opened the door. With her short brown hair and tiny hands, she was an optical-illusion woman, mysteriously making everyone around her seem larger than they really were. Paxton was five-ten and had at least eight inches and fifty pounds on Kirsty. She hated how she towered over her, but she never let it show, never stooped or wore flats around her. That would be shifting the balance of power. "Hi, Pax. Come in. You're a little late."

"I know. Sorry. Colin came home early. We were

catching up," she said as she entered and followed Kirsty to the living room. "How are you?"

Kirsty rambled on about her perfect husband and her lovably unruly boys and her fabulous part-time job as a real estate agent.

The twenty-four members sat in folding chairs set up in straight rows across the living room. Some had snack plates in their laps, full of scoops of lemon-chicken salad, lemon and broccoli mini-quiches, and tiny lemon meringue cups from the buffet table. There was a small table at the back of the room where three teenage girls, dressed in party clothes, whispered among themselves. They were called the Springs. These were the daughters of committee members being molded to take their mothers' places when the time came. This was a young woman's club. After a certain age, it was understood that you were no longer welcome, and that your daughter was expected to take your place. As a rule, rich Southern women did not like to be surpassed in either need or beauty. The exception was with their daughters. Daughters of the South were to their mothers what tributaries were to the main rivers they flowed into: their source of immovable strength.

Paxton smiled at the girls as she walked over to them and gave them small bags of chocolate. As president, she always gave the girls gifts at meetings, to make them feel included. They all hugged her, and she squeezed them back. She'd assumed she'd be married and have kids by this age, that she would be grooming her own daughter for this, as her friends were doing. She wanted it so much she would dream about it sometimes, and then she would wake up with the skin at her wrists and neck red from the scratchy lace of the wedding gown she'd dreamed of wearing. But she'd never felt anything for the men she'd dated, nothing beyond her own desperation. And her desire to marry wasn't strong enough, would *never* be strong enough, to allow her to marry a man she didn't love.

She skipped the food, as she always did because of the looks some of her friends gave her, eyeing her wide hips, and went to the front of the room, saying her hellos along the way. A strange breeze slithered by her, which sounded like whispers of secrets. She shook it off distractedly.

She took out her notebooks at the podium. "All right, everyone, come to order. We have a lot to discuss. RSVPs for the gala are pouring in. And Moira has a request that the Madam open to overnight guests early, so that some elderly attendees coming in from out of town can stay there the evening of the gala. But first, the reading of minutes from the last meeting. Stacey?"

Stacey Herbst stood and flipped through her notebook. She had recently started dying her hair red and, though everyone told her they missed her brown hair, the truth was she looked better as a redhead. But she would probably go back to brown soon. What people thought meant too much to her.

Stacey opened her mouth to read the minutes but, amazingly, what came out was, "I steal lipstick every time I go to the drugstore. I can't help myself. I just drop a tube in my purse and walk out. I love that none of you know, that it's a secret I keep from you."

She slapped her hand over her mouth.

Paxton's brows rose. But before she could say anything, Honor Redford, who had been president of the club before Paxton had taken over, blurted out, "Ever since my husband lost his job I've been afraid I won't be able to afford the club dues, and none of you will like me anymore."

Moira Kinley turned to the woman sitting next to her and said, "You know why I like going places in public with you? Because I'm prettier, and you make me feel better about myself."

"I had that new addition built just because I knew it would make you jealous."

"I really did have a boob job."

"I know you have a bladder problem, but I tell everyone that the reason you have to go to the bathroom so often is because you're bulimic."

Now everyone was talking at once, and each thing they said was more outrageous than the last. Paxton stared at them impatiently. She thought at first that they were playing a joke on her, because some of them thought it was funny to try to get a rise out of her, as she was notoriously unflustered. But then she realized that everyone looked panicked, their eyes like horses running scared. It was as if everything they were secretly thinking had suddenly been given a voice, and they were powerless to stop it.

"Order," Paxton said. "Everyone come to order." This had no effect. The din escalated. Paxton stepped up onto her chair and clapped loudly, then yelled, "Come to order! What is the matter with you?"

The noise dissipated as everyone looked up at her. She stepped down. She could feel it now, an uneasiness creeping along her skin. She blinked a few times, because things suddenly seemed distorted, like looking at your reflection in a spoon. She had to stop herself from blurting out that she was in love with someone she shouldn't be, something she'd never admitted to anyone. But now she was aching to say it. God, it felt like she would die, that she would choke on it, if she didn't get it out.

She swallowed and managed to say instead, "Kirsty, I think something might be wrong with your air conditioner. I think we're being affected by fumes."

"At least I have my own house," Kirsty murmured as she got up and crossed the room to the thermostat. "At least I don't live in my parents' pool house."

"Excuse me?" Paxton said.

"Wh . . . I . . ." Kirsty stammered. "I didn't mean to say that out loud."

Paxton rallied everyone and got them to open all the windows and take deep breaths. The sticky July heat crawling into the room quickly made everyone sweat through their light summer powders. The meeting was called to order, and the list of things needing to be addressed was checked off, but Paxton could tell some women just weren't listening. It was close to ten o'clock when the meeting finally ended. Everyone kissed one another's cheeks and rushed off to their respective houses to make sure everything was all right, that homes hadn't burned down, that husbands hadn't left, that their best dresses still fit.

Paxton sat in her car in Kirsty's driveway, watching cars peel out, thinking to herself, *What in the hell just happened here?*

Instead of going home, Paxton drove to Sebastian Rogers's house. She saw that his lights were still on, so she pulled into his driveway.

When Sebastian moved back to Walls of Water to take over old Dr. Kostovo's dental practice last year, he'd also bought Dr. Kostovo's house, because Dr. K was retiring to Nevada to get away from the moist Walls of Water air that bothered his arthritis. It was a dark stone house with a decorative stone turret. It was called Shade Tree Cottage, and Sebastian once told Paxton that he liked the drama of the place, that he liked to pretend he was living in an episode of *Dark Shadows.*

She knocked on his door. Moments later, Sebastian opened it. "Hello, beautiful," he said, and opened the door farther for her to enter. "I didn't expect to see you tonight."

"I just wanted to say hi," she said as she walked in, and the words sounded lame, even to her, as if there necessarily had to be an excuse, even though she knew he didn't mind her stopping by.

She walked to the living room and sat on the couch, where he'd obviously been watching television. Judging by the outside, one would expect swords and coats of arms on the walls inside, but Sebastian had instead made the interior light and comfortable. He had moved

back not long after she'd decided against buying the
townhouse, and she'd enjoyed watching this place turn
into his own. She even secretly envied his independence sometimes. She took off her shoes and tucked
her feet under her as Sebastian sat beside her and
crossed his legs at the knees. He was wearing draw-
string pants and a T-shirt. His feet were bare, his toe-
nails neatly trimmed.

Sebastian was a beautiful man, his face as delicate as
a John Donne poem. Everyone presumed he was gay,
but no one really knew for sure. He neither confirmed
nor denied it, not in high school, and not now. Paxton
was fairly certain, though, that she was the only person
here to have ever seen proof. In high school he'd been
thin and fair, wore eyeliner and long coats, and carried
a satchel when everyone else in school had L.L.Bean
backpacks. He'd been hard to miss. That's why he'd
caught her eye in the Asheville Mall their senior year.
Asheville was about an hour outside of Walls of Water,
and Paxton and her friends went there nearly every Saturday. Sebastian had been in the food court with at least
a half-dozen other flamboyant teenage boys, boys not
from Walls of Water. This was a different crowd, one
not seen in small towns. She and her friends had been
walking by when she'd spotted him. Suddenly, one of
the exotic boys with black spiky hair and elbow-length
black-and-white fingerless gloves leaned over the table
and kissed Sebastian full on the mouth, deeply. At some
point during the kiss, Sebastian had opened his eyes
and seen her. Still kissing the boy, his eyes followed her

as she'd walked away. She couldn't remember ever seeing something as bold and seductive.

Thinking back to that kiss, it seemed so unlike him
now. He was very controlled these days, almost asexual
in the sharply tailored suits he wore to work, complete
with silk ties so smooth they caught light.

"How was your day?" he asked, propping his elbow
on the back of the couch, so close he almost touched
her.

"Okay, I guess." She reached over and lifted his half-
empty wineglass from the coffee table and took a sip.

He tilted his head. "Just okay?"

"The bright spot was that Colin got here earlier than
expected. The landscaping at the Madam is going to be
done on time for sure now. But the club meeting
tonight was so *odd*. I've never seen anything like it.
There's still so much to do for the gala, and suddenly
everyone seems distracted."

"How so?"

She paused, thinking about it. "Whenever I would
get too nosy as a child, my grandmother would say,
*When you learn someone else's secret, your own secrets
aren't safe. Dig up one, release them all*. That's what the
meeting was like. Everyone was admitting things, secret things. And once they started, it was like they
couldn't stop."

He smiled. "I'm confused. Isn't that what the meetings are all about? Gossip?"

"Not like this," she said. "Trust me."

"Then do tell," he said, raising his eyebrows. "What

secrets have the society ladies been keeping? What's *your* secret?"

Paxton tried to laugh, but it made her head hurt. She rubbed her forehead. "I don't have secrets."

He kept his eyebrows raised.

She *had* to admit to something now. But definitely not what she'd almost admitted at the meeting. "I'm dreading telling my grandmother about the gala. I promised my mother I would do it tomorrow morning, but I don't want to. I really, *really* don't want to. And I feel terrible about it. Nana Osgood helped found the club. It was wrong to keep this from her for so long. But she's just so . . . ."

Sebastian nodded. He knew. "Do you want me to go with you?"

"No. She treats you horribly." Ever since she and Sebastian had started spending their Sundays together—something she looked forward to all week, like counting down the days to Christmas—he'd been coming with her to her weekly visits with her grandmother on Sunday evenings. She wasn't going to make him come with her on a weekday, too. That was too much to ask of anyone.

"She treats everyone horribly, darling." He reached over and took the wineglass from her and set it down, then took her hand in his. "Let go of that tightfisted control. You don't have to do everything yourself." He looked her in the eye and said, "I'll go with you to see your grandmother tomorrow."

"Really?"

"You know I'd do anything for you."

She put his hand to her warm cheek and closed her
eyes. His skin was cool and soft. He'd once told her
that if she washed her hands as many times as he did in
a day, moisturizer would become her best friend, too.

She realized what she was doing, and her eyes flew
open. She let go of his hand and stood, fumbling with
her shoes. "I should go," she said, while trying to wedge
her feet back into her strappy heels. "Thanks for letting
me vent."

"You're such a ball of energy. Do you actually sleep?"

She gave him a weak smile. "Occasionally."

He slowly uncrossed his legs, watching her thoughtfully as he stood. The moment they'd met again when
he'd moved back, just by chance after her book club
meeting at Hartley's Tea Room last year, Paxton had
felt a sting she'd been completely unprepared for, like a
shock of electricity. She hadn't recognized him at first,
she'd known only that he was staggeringly beautiful, almost otherworldly, and she'd wondered what he was
doing in Walls of Water. She had resolved to call
around and find out who he was as she'd unlocked her
car door, still staring at him as he'd walked to his car,
parked a few spaces down. He'd opened his door and
tossed the bag he'd been carrying from the Slightly
Foxed Bookstore inside, then he'd turned to see her
staring at him. He'd stared back, then smiled slightly
and said, "Hello, Paxton," which had blown her to
pieces. He'd had to remind her that they had gone to
school together. They'd ended up back in Hartley's Tea
Room, talking for hours. By the time they'd parted ways
that afternoon, she'd been done for. And the reality of

it would still catch her off guard. No matter how many times she told herself that nothing good could come of this, that she was just setting herself up, she couldn't seem to help her feelings for him.

"Good night, lovely," he said. He reached out and petted her hair almost apologetically. And that's when it hit her so hard it made her chest hurt. *He knew.*

Appalled, she turned to the door. How long had he known? All along? Or had she done something recently to make him suspect? My God, what an awful night this had turned out to be. It felt like the universe was playing tricks.

"Pax? What's wrong?" he asked, following her.

"Nothing. I'm fine. I'll see you tomorrow morning," she tried to say brightly as she walked outside into a cloak of humid darkness.

And she could have sworn she heard the whisper of someone's laughter.

THREE

Code of Outcasts

Willa heard the knock at her door just as she was taking the last load out of the dryer that evening. She had a feeling she knew who it was, but with all her windows closed and the air conditioner on, she'd thought her prickly neighbors wouldn't be able to hear it when she'd cranked up Bruce Springsteen.

She set the load of clothes on her kitchen table, skipping her usual ritual of burying her face in the warm laundry, and walked through the shotgun-style house to the front door.

This was one of the drawbacks to living in an old neighborhood with houses so close together. But Willa had inherited this, her childhood home, when her father had passed away almost seven years ago. A mortgage-free house was nothing to sneeze at, especially considering she had finally paid off the astronomical credit card debt she'd acquired in college. Walls of Water had an unusually high number per capita of wealthy residents, and when she was younger she used to hate not being one of them. It had been a heady feeling to suddenly have such easy access to cash in college, to run fast and loose with it like she'd always wanted. Her father had died before he'd found out how deep in debt she'd gotten.

She was now the debt-free owner of a business and a home, all thanks to her father, who had left her the house and made her the beneficiary of his life insurance policy. Being an adult was important to him. She owed him this. This was her penance for causing him and her grandmother so much grief, for her astounding inability to tamp down all her restless energy when she was younger and live the quiet life they wanted.

Springsteen was singing "I'm on Fire" when she opened the door. She looked up, and the man on her doorstep said, "We meet again."

Any sound that might have been forming in her throat disappeared. When she opened her mouth, all that came out was breath filled with dissolved words.

"You ran away so fast today that you forgot this." He held out the invitation.

She took it quickly and, inexplicably, hid it behind her back.

He put his hands in his pockets. He was still wearing the same pants and dress shirt from earlier, now dry and resembling crumpled paper. The sharp light from

the globe beside her door was making him squint a little, causing small lines to crinkle around his eyes. He
stared at her a moment before he said, "I took the
blame for all your pranks in high school. The least you
can do is invite me in."

That snapped her out of it. "You didn't take the
blame, you took the *credit*," she said.

He smiled. "So you do remember me."

Of course she remembered him. It was what made
being caught on Jackson Hill all the more embarrassing. Even though she'd never paid much attention to
Colin in school, everyone knew who he was. He was an
Osgood. But he'd always been eclipsed by his popular
and headstrong twin sister. Not that he seemed to
mind. He probably could have been as popular as Paxton was, but he'd never seemed as interested as his sister in running for student body president every year
and joining three million different clubs. He'd mostly
hung out with boys who wore pastel polo shirts and
played golf on the weekends. He'd seemed destined to
come back after college and take his father's place as
King of the Links, but for some reason he stayed away.
She had no idea why.

Willa hadn't intentionally tried to frame him for her
pranks in high school. At the beginning of their senior
year, she'd snuck out one night and put a quote by poet
Ogden Nash on the school's marquee. CANDY IS DANDY
BUT LIQUOR IS QUICKER. She'd overheard Colin say it—
he'd been quoting it all day—and she'd thought it was
funny. What she didn't know was that Colin had just
turned in an independent-study essay on Ogden Nash

the day before, so she had inadvertently pointed the finger at him. No one could ever prove it was Colin, and his parents had made absolutely certain that Colin was never held accountable, but every prank Willa had pulled up until then, and every one after, had been credited to him. He had earned the respect of being the Walls of Water High School Joker, the hero of students, the bane of the teachers' existence. It was only when Willa had actually been caught, three weeks before graduation, that everyone had realized it was her, not Colin.

"Are you going to let me in or not? The suspense is killing me."

She sighed as she stepped back. When he entered, she closed the door behind him, then she stepped over to her iPod speakers next to her computer and turned the volume down, before Springsteen could sound any sexier. She turned to see Colin walking around, absently running his hand over the back of her super-soft couch. It was that kind of couch. You just *had* to touch it. After almost seven years, it was the first new thing she'd bought for the house, and it had been delivered just days ago. It was expensive and impractical, and she felt suitably guilty, but she was ridiculously in love with it.

"No one told me you'd moved back," Colin said.

"Why would they?"

He shook his head as if he didn't know the answer. "How long have you been here?"

"Since my dad died."

Colin's shoulders dropped a little. "I was sorry to hear about what happened." Her father had been hit and killed trying to help someone change a tire on the interstate during what would have been Willa's senior year in college, if she hadn't flunked out. Another thing her father hadn't known about. "He was a great teacher. I had him for chemistry in eleventh grade. He had a dinner for his AP students here at his house once."

"Yes, I remember." She'd hated those dinners, actually having kids come to her house to see how she lived. She would hide in her room and pretend to be sick. There was nothing wrong with the house, it was just old and small, nothing like the mansions half the kids lived in.

"I've thought a lot about you over the years, what you were doing, what mischief you were getting yourself into." He paused. "I had no idea you'd been here the whole time."

She just stared at him, wondering why it mattered.

He circled the living room again, looking around, then didn't seem to know what else to do, so he sat on the couch with a weary sigh. He ran his fingers through his dark hair. His hands were large. He was a big man, with a big presence. No one had seemed to notice that in high school. His time away had changed him, had given him a confidence, an air of independence, that he didn't have before. "So what are you doing these days, Willa Jackson?"

"I own a sporting goods store on National Street." There. That sounded responsible, didn't it? Normal and practical.

"What do you do for fun?"

She gave him a funny look. What kind of question was that? "Laundry," she answered, deadpan.

"Married?" he asked. "Kids?"

"No."

"So no progeny to teach how to TP the high school lawn, or decorate the teachers' cars with peanut butter, or put scandalous quotes on the school marquee, or switch the items in the school lockers of the entire graduating class?" He laughed. "That was a classic. It had to have taken all night."

It was like it was a fond memory to him. But she'd purposely not revisited her pranks in years. And she hadn't given Colin a second thought. Now, suddenly, she was remembering the look on his face when she'd been escorted out of the school by police after pulling the fire alarm. The whole school was out on the lawn. *It was her,* they'd whispered. *Willa Jackson was the Walls of Water High School Joker!* Colin Osgood had looked completely poleaxed. Though whether it was because it was her or because he couldn't take credit for her pranks anymore, she didn't know.

They stared at each other from across the room. She watched as his eyes traveled down her body, and she was about to call him on it when he said, "So, are you going?" He nodded to the invitation still in her hand. "To the gala?"

She looked down as if surprised to find the invitation there. She put it on the computer table, giving it a dirty look, as if this was all the invitation's fault. "No."

"Why not?"

"Because it doesn't have anything to do with me."

"So you only go to parties that have something to do with you? Your birthday party, for example." After a short silence, he frowned and said, "That sounded funnier in my head. Sorry. Everything suddenly starts to seem funny when you've been up for forty-eight hours. I laughed at a speed limit sign on my way over here. I have no idea why."

He was sleep-drunk. That explained a lot of things. "Why have you been up for forty-eight hours?"

"Couldn't sleep on the flight from Japan. And I've been trying to stay awake all day so I could go to bed at a regular hour and not get hopelessly lost in the time difference."

She looked toward the window. "Did someone drive you here?"

"No."

She met his eyes. They were dark and unnerving and very, very tired. "Are you okay to drive home?" she asked seriously.

He smiled. "That was a very responsible thing to ask."

"Let me get you some coffee."

"If you insist. But the old Willa would have found some way to take advantage of this situation."

"You have no idea who the old Willa was," she said.

"Neither do you, obviously."

Without another word, she turned and went to the kitchen, where she managed to spill both the coffee grounds and the water. She just wanted to get her father's old percolator going so she could give Colin a jolt of caffeine and have him be on his way.

"Do you go up to the Blue Ridge Madam often?" Colin called from the living room.

"No," she answered. Of course he'd get around to that.

"So you weren't planning a prank for, say, the big gala?" He actually said that hopefully.

"Oh, for God's sake," Willa mumbled.

Leaning against the kitchen counter, she watched the percolator as it gurgled and took its time. When it had finally made enough for a single serving, she poured some into a cup and took it to the living room.

He was still sitting on her gray microsuede couch, his hands on his knees, his head resting back against the cushions.

"Oh, no," she said, panicking as she set the cup down on the end table. "No, no, no. Colin, wake up."

He didn't stir.

She reached over and touched his shoulder. "Colin, I have your coffee. Wake up and drink some." She shook his shoulder. "Colin!"

His eyes opened, and he looked at her, a little unfocused. "What happened to you? You were the bravest person I knew," he murmured. Then he closed his eyes again.

"Colin?" She watched for a telltale flutter of his long eyelashes, thinking maybe he was playing some game with her. "Colin?"

Nothing.

She stood there for a moment, stunned. Just as she was about to turn, she caught a whiff of something sweet. She inhaled deeply, instinctively wanting to savor it, but then she nearly choked when it landed on her tongue with a bitter taste. It was so strong she actually made a face.

That, her grandmother had described to her once after making a particularly bad lemon cream pie, was exactly what regret tasted like.

The thick morning mist in Walls of Water, common because of the nearby waterfalls, was famous in itself. There wasn't a single store on National Street that didn't sell those touristy Jars of Fog, gray-glass jars visitors could take home with them to remind them of their stay. Willa figured it was a lot like living near the ocean. When you see it every day, sometimes you wonder what the big deal is.

The mist was just beginning to disappear with the rising heat as Willa got into her Wrangler the next morning and drove toward the nursing home. Thankfully, Colin had gotten up and left sometime during the night, taking his disappointment that she wasn't still secretly pulling pranks on the town, that she wasn't still eighteen, with him.

She wished he'd never come to see her. She was doing the right thing being here. She'd grown up. The whole point of being here was so she *didn't* disappoint people anymore.

"Hi, Grandmother Georgie," Willa said brightly when she got to the nursing home and walked into her room. Her grandmother had already been dressed and put in her wheelchair. She was sitting, slightly stooped, by the window. The morning sun on her white hair and pale face made her seem almost translucent. She'd been a beautiful woman in her day, with wide eyes, high cheekbones, and a long, thin nose. Sometimes you could still catch sight of that beauty, and it was like looking through enchanted glass.

Her grandmother had been showing the first signs of dementia when Willa left for college. That's when Willa's father had moved her in with him, into Willa's old bedroom. Two years later, she'd had a stroke, and he'd been forced to move her to the nursing home. Willa knew the decision wasn't easy for him, but he'd managed to get her into the nicest facility in the area. After her father died, Willa took his place coming to visit her, because she knew that was what he would have wanted. He'd adored his mother, and pleasing her had been his life's ambition.

Willa had always thought her grandmother was sweet, but she'd been one of those people with invisible thorns, preventing others from getting too close. Georgie Jackson had been a nervous, watchful person, not at all frivolous, which Willa had found extraordinary, considering how rich the Jacksons had once been. But after her family had lost their money, Georgie had worked as a maid for various wealthy families in town until she was well into her seventies.

She'd always been quiet, like Willa's father. Willa's mother had been the loud one in the family, and Willa could still remember her laugh, a sweet staccato sound like embers popping. She'd been a receptionist at a local law office, but she'd died when Willa was six. That had marked the phase when Willa used to like to play dead. She used to pose herself on the couch, completely soaked, as if she'd drowned there. She would drape herself awkwardly across the car hood, as if she'd been hit. Her favorite death was Death By Spoons, in which she would lie on the kitchen floor, douse herself with ketchup, and stick spoons under her armpits. At that age, Willa hadn't understood death, hadn't seen it as a bad thing if it had happened to someone as nice as her mother, and frankly, she'd been fascinated by it.

Once her grandmother had caught her having an imaginary conversation with her mother, and had immediately opened all the windows and burned sage. *Ghosts are horrible things,* she'd said. *You don't talk to them. You keep them away.* It had hurt Willa, and it had taken a long time to forgive her grandmother for denying her a link to her mother, for making her scared of it, no matter how silly.

All those superstitions were gone from her grandmother's memory now. Her grandmother didn't even recognize Willa anymore, but Willa knew she liked the melody of voices, even though she no longer understood the words. So this was what Willa did several times a week; she came and talked about what was on the news, what the trees looked like this time of year, what was selling in her shop right now, what improvements she was making to her dad's house. She told her grandmother about the new couch, but not about Colin.

She talked until the food-service lady brought Georgie's breakfast, then Willa helped feed her. After

her tray had been cleared, she gently washed her
grandmother's face and sat back beside her.

She hesitated a few moments before she brought the
invitation from her back pocket. "I've been debating
whether or not I should tell you about this. There's a
party at the Blue Ridge Madam next month. The
Women's Society Club is celebrating the formation of
the club. Paxton Osgood wants to honor you at the
party, which I guess is nice. But you never talked about
it. I don't know if it really meant anything to you. If I
thought it did, I would go. But I just don't know."

Willa looked down at the invitation and did the math
for the first time. She realized her grandmother had
been only seventeen when she'd helped form the club.
That had been the year her family had lost the Blue
Ridge Madam, the year she'd given birth to Willa's father.

It pained Willa to think of it now, but she'd never
been particularly proud of being a Jackson when she
was younger. But the older she got, the more she came
to appreciate just how hard her family had worked to
support themselves, how no one but her had ever cast
their eyes down in shame at what they had lost. Willa
had already faced and accepted that her grandmother
could no longer tell her things she wanted to know
about her family, that she'd missed all the opportunities
to ask her when she was clear-minded, or to ask her father while he was alive. But times like this she still felt
it acutely, all the *I love you*s she should have said but
didn't, the things she wished she could go back in time

and change, how she should have made them proud of her instead of constantly worrying them.

Willa looked up from the invitation and was surprised to find that Georgie had turned her head and her light gray eyes, the same shade as Willa's, were looking directly at her, as if she'd recognized something familiar in what Willa had said. It hadn't happened in literally years, and Willa was so surprised that her heart picked up speed.

Willa leaned forward. "What is it, Grandmother Georgie? The Blue Ridge Madam? The Women's Society Club?"

Georgie's left side was rendered useless from the stroke, so she moved her right hand over to Willa's. She tried to get her mouth to move, to form words.

It took a few tries before Willa recognized one word: *peach*.

"Peach? You want peaches?"

Her grandmother's face suddenly went slack, as if she'd forgotten. She turned back to the window.

"Okay, Grandmother Georgie," she said as she stood and kissed her head. "I'll make sure you have some peaches."

She wrapped a shawl around her grandmother's shoulders and promised her that she'd be back to see her soon.

With one last look, she turned and left the room.

It was silly to expect something profound. That she was trying to communicate at all was enough.

She stopped at the nurses' station to see if there were

any medical notes, then asked if her grandmother could have peaches with her next meal.

She put on her sunglasses and walked outside into the razor-sharp sunshine, crossing the wide brick patio toward the parking lot. The sun was already glinting in hot metallic waves off car windshields, which was why she didn't see that someone was approaching her until she was only a few steps away.

It was Paxton Osgood, wearing a cute pink dress and gorgeous shoes. She was tall like her brother, but had wide curves, as if one of her angular French ancestors had scandalized everyone by marrying a pretty stout milkmaid, and several generations later, Paxton was the result. Beside her was a man with blond hair and fair skin. He was in a tailored suit that shouldn't have looked so good on someone that slim. But it did. He was beautiful in the most unusual way, one of those people you couldn't quite figure out which side of masculine or feminine they fell on.

Not knowing what Colin had told his sister about last night, or what hard feelings Paxton still harbored for that time Willa faked a love letter from Paxton to Robbie Roberts, Willa wasn't exactly sure what to expect from her by way of greeting, or even if she was going to greet her at all.

She definitely wasn't expecting Paxton to smile and say, "Willa! Hello! I'm so glad I ran into you. Are you here in the mornings, then? That's why I never see you. Did you get my note about wanting to do something special for our grandmothers at the gala?"

Willa self-consciously patted at her wild, wavy hair

because Paxton's hair was in her trademark chignon. She was always so polished. "My grandmother isn't well enough to attend," Willa said. "She doesn't even remember me, much less the club."

"Yes, I know. And I'm sorry," Paxton said. "What I was thinking of doing was honoring her through you. That you could accept a gift for her."

"I . . . think I have a previous engagement that evening," Willa said.

"Oh," Paxton said, obviously surprised. There was an awkward pause.

Sebastian cleared his throat. "Hello, Willa. Nice to see you again. It's been a while."

"Sebastian. I heard you'd taken over Dr. Kostovo's practice." Sebastian Rogers reinforced her belief that reinvention was not just a nice theory. It really did happen. Back in high school, her peers would sometimes forget she was there because she was normally so quiet during school, but Sebastian wasn't nearly as lucky. Willa had the power to be invisible, something someone who looked like Sebastian could never be. He had endured constant taunts. And yet here he was, a DMD in a suit that probably cost more than a year's worth of her Jeep payments. "The last time I saw you, you had on eyeliner and a purple trench coat."

"The last time I saw you, you were being arrested for pulling the fire alarm."

"Touché. Come by Au Naturel on National Street sometime. You can have coffee on the house."

"Perhaps I will. You were a patient of Dr. Kostovo's,

weren't you? I expect you to continue to come for regular cleanings."

"You're the dental police now?"

He lifted one eyebrow seriously. "Yes, I am."

Willa laughed, then realized Paxton was looking at her curiously. Her laughter fading, Willa looked from Paxton to Sebastian, then back again.

"Well, I've got to go," she finally said.

"Goodbye, Willa," Sebastian said as she walked away.

Paxton didn't say anything.

⁂

Paxton watched Sebastian from the corner of her eye as they walked down the hallway toward her grand-mother's room. Her steps were heavy in her heels, but his were whisper-light in his Italian loafers. Even the bouquet of hydrangeas he was carrying didn't crinkle. "I don't remember you and Willa being particularly close in high school. Were you?"

"No," he said simply.

"She seemed happier to see you than me."

"The code of outcasts," he said with a smile. "You wouldn't understand." Before Paxton could ask, they reached her grandmother's door. "Ready to see the dragon lady?"

"No," Paxton said.

"I'm here for you." Sebastian put his arm around her waist and gave her a comforting squeeze before drop-ping his arm.

They walked in together, and Paxton cautiously approached her grandmother's bed. Every time she got near her, she could feel her skin start to burn. She'd been afraid of this woman all her life, something she'd never told anyone. She would look at her grandmother and feel absolute terror that she was going to turn into her one day. "Nana Osgood?" she said gently. "It's me, Paxton. Are you awake?"

Without opening her eyes, Agatha said, "The fact that you had to ask should have given you a clue."

"I'm here with Sebastian this morning."

She finally opened her eyes. "Oh, the fancy man."

Paxton sighed, but Sebastian smiled and winked at her. "I brought you some hydrangeas, Agatha," he said. "Your favorite."

"You don't have to tell me they're my favorite. I know they're my favorite. But my question is, why are you bringing flowers to a blind woman? I can't see them. I keep telling you, I want chocolates. Food is my last re-maining pleasure."

"Nana, you know Mama doesn't want you to have too many sweets."

"Your mama doesn't know anything. Give me my teeth."

"Where are they?" Paxton asked.

"On the table where they always are," Agatha said as she sat up. "Honestly, it's not like we don't do this every time you visit. Why are you here so early, anyway? This isn't even your day to come see me."

"I have something wonderful to tell you about the Blue Ridge Madam," Paxton said, looking to the bedside table for her grandmother's teeth.

"There's nothing wonderful about the Blue Ridge Madam. Stay away from it. It's haunted. Give me my teeth."

Paxton started to panic. "Your teeth aren't here."

"Of course they are." Agatha threw her covers off as she stood and nudged Paxton out of the way. She patted the tabletop with her hands, her gummy mouth agape. "Where are they? Someone stole my teeth! Thieves!" she screamed. "Thieves!"

"I'll just put these in some water," Sebastian said as he took a Waterford crystal vase from the bureau and went into the attached bathroom. Seconds later, he leaned out and said, "Darling?"

Paxton was now on her knees, looking under her grandmother's bed, while Agatha continued to scream. She looked up to find him desperately trying to suppress a laugh. She loved that he didn't let her grandmother get to him. She loved that he was willing to go through this with her, that she didn't have to hide how horrible Agatha was. If he could live with her secret, then she could live with him knowing. Nothing was going to happen between them. If they just carried on like always, everything would be okay.

"I believe I've located Agatha's teeth," he said.

After Paxton and the fancy man left, Agatha Osgood sat in her chair in her room, her lips set, her fingers pinching nervously at her cardigan, which she could only assume matched her dress. Macular degeneration had all but taken her eyesight. But she knew where all her fur-

niture was in her room, and it was soft and comfortable. Someone told her the upholstery was in a blue
hydrangea pattern, which, when the light hit it right,
she could almost make out. She also had her own
miniature refrigerator that her family kept stocked with
things she liked. She still enjoyed food, so that helped
a little, even if they didn't give her as much chocolate
as she wanted. This wasn't such a bad place, she supposed. It was, in fact, the best facility around, as was
reflected in the cost. Not that Agatha minded anything
about money. That's what happens when you have too
much of it. It becomes like dust, something that constantly moves around you but that you never actually
touch.

She'd thought her family consulted her on things.
She'd thought that, as matriarch, her opinion was still
relevant. That was the impression they gave her when
they visited. But she realized now just how coddled she
was. This place lulled its residents into thinking that
this was all there was to the world anymore. It shrank
everything down, Alice in Wonderlandly. It was startling
to her that there was still a world outside these walls,
one that went on turning even when she wasn't in it.

She couldn't believe her family had actually bought
the Blue Ridge Madam. All those years of carefully
constructing the rumors of ghosts, of making every
child, and most adults, afraid of the Madam, of watching it crumble, year after year, waiting for the time
when it would finally collapse and it and everything
that had happened there would disappear, had been for
naught.

And if that wasn't bad enough, Paxton was planning a big gala there, celebrating the formation of the Women's Society Club. Agatha had tried everything she could to get Paxton to stop it, to cancel it. She'd said hateful things she didn't mean and made threats she couldn't keep, but nothing was going to stop it. Paxton was in control of the club now, and Agatha felt her lack of power acutely.

Those silly girls had no idea what they were really celebrating. They had no idea what it took to bring Agatha and her friends together seventy-five years ago. The Women's Society Club had been about supporting one another, about banding together to protect one another because no one else would. But it had turned into an ugly beast, a means by which rich ladies could congratulate themselves by giving money to the poor. And Agatha had let it happen. All her life, it seemed, she was making up for things she let happen.

She knew it wasn't a coincidence that the club would be celebrating in the Madam. There was no such thing as coincidence. It was fate. Looking at it objectively, it even had a cruel sort of symmetry. The reason they'd started the club in the first place had to do with the Madam. It was just a matter of time now before it was all going to come to light. Secrets never stay buried, no matter how hard you try. That's what Georgie had always been afraid of.

She got up and walked out of her room, counting her steps to the nurses' station. She could hear the morning nurse's voice there as she approached. She was young. Too young. She sounded like she should still be playing hopscotch with her best friends. Why were girls in such a hurry to grow up? Agatha would never understand. Childhood was magical. Leaving it behind was a magnificent loss.

"Hello, Mrs. Osgood," the nurse said, in a tone that tried but fell short of pleasant. Agatha inspired this in all the help here. She wasn't sure when it had happened, but sometime in the past ten years, she'd discovered that it made her feel better to make other people as miserable as she was. It was the help who hid her teeth in the bathroom this morning, where the fancy man had found them. She was sure of it. It was a give-and-take she'd played with the staff for years now. "What can I do for you?"

"If I need your help, I'll ask for it," Agatha snapped as she walked by. She walked to the third hallway, her papery fingertips trailing along the walls as she counted the doors to Georgie Jackson's room. When Georgie's son Ham had come to her and asked for Agatha's help in getting Georgie a place here in the home, Agatha had given him the money without hesitation. All she'd ever wanted was to help Georgie, to make up for the one time when Georgie had needed her the most and Agatha had turned her back on her . . . the one time that had changed everything. Agatha kept tabs on how Georgie was being treated, but she rarely visited Georgie here. Georgie wouldn't have liked it. She would have said, *You have your side, I have mine. That's the way it has to be now.*

When she reached the room, all Agatha could make out was a dark form haloed by the morning sun. Georgie looked like a hole Agatha could fall into.

Agatha mourned for a lot of things she'd lost, but lately this was the loss she felt the most—the loss of friendship. She missed her eyesight. She missed her husband. She missed her mother and father. But those girls she grew up with were such an important part of her life. If her old friends all appeared to her now, she would protect them with her last breath, which of course was too little, too late. The way it had always been. They were gone, all except for Georgie, who was suspended here in life only by a thin, glittering thread.

She walked over to Georgie and sat beside her. "It's finally happening," Agatha whispered.

Georgie—sweet, innocent Georgie—turned to her and said, "Peach."

Agatha fumbled around until she found Georgie's hand, and then held it in her own. "Yes," Agatha said. "It's still there."

But the question was, for how long?

FOUR

Wish Lists

Colin sat in the corner café of Au Naturel Sporting Goods, nursing his cappuccino and staring out the large store window at the cars going by. Because this road led directly to the entrance of Cataract National Forest, there was a lot of traffic. This side of town had a completely different feel to it, hectic and slightly superficial. It had been a long time since he'd been here, but nothing much had changed, like the fact that locals rarely came to National Street because they considered it too touristy. The long rows of brick buildings were old, but the shops they housed were hip and new, and most were owned by transplants.

As much as he didn't like acknowledging it, he was still connected to this place, if just by memory. He'd seen a lot of the world in his work. Urban landscaping wasn't about homogenizing cities but drawing from their heritage, and he was one of the best landscape architects in the business. Learning about new cultures, traveling to new places, not staying in one place too long—it was exactly what he wanted to be doing. But then he would come home, usually only when forced by guilt from his mother or, in this instance, a request for help from his sister, who never asked for help, and he would feel a strange sensation, like his feet growing heavy. It was as if he was sinking back into the root system of this place. And he didn't want to be that Colin anymore, the one planted here, the one pruned to exactly the size and shape everyone expected him to be.

He heard the bell over the door ring, and he turned.

Willa Jackson had just walked in. She was wearing jeans over black cowboy boots and a black sleeveless top that crisscrossed over her bare shoulders. Her honey-brown hair was wavy in a way that was no curl and all volume. It'd been much longer in high school, and she'd always worn it in a messy braid. Actually, he really didn't know if she'd always worn it like that, it was just how he remembered it the last time he saw her, walking out of the school.

Now her hair ended just below her ears and she parted it on the side, catching the hair at one temple with a sparkly barrette. He liked it because it was spunky, and it suited the image of what he thought she'd become. He didn't realize he'd gotten it so wrong. *Surely* he couldn't have gotten it so wrong. Because if he was wrong about Willa, his inspiration, then maybe he was wrong about his own decisions, too.

The girl who'd earlier made him the cappuccino excused herself from talking to a customer and walked over to Willa. He could hear her say, "Someone is here to see you."

"Who?" Willa asked.

"I don't know. He came in about an hour ago and asked for you. I told him you'd be here soon, so he's sitting in the café, waiting for you. *Cappuccino with one raw sugar*," she said in a lower voice, reciting his order as if it was confidential information, some secret she was revealing about him.

Willa turned to walk toward the café but stopped when she saw him. She turned away quickly, which made him smile.

"What?" the dark-haired girl asked. "Who is he?"

"Colin Osgood," Willa said.

"Related to Paxton?"

"Her brother."

"Do you hate him, too?" the girl asked.

"Stop it. I don't hate them," Willa murmured before turning back around and walking over to him. She stopped at his table and gave him a polite smile. "I see you made it home alive."

"Yes. And I want to apologize for last night. I haven't been that tired in a long time." He rubbed his eyes with one hand. He felt like a ghost of his former self, like someone could reach for him and get only air. "I could probably sleep for days more."

"Then what are you doing here?"

"Pit stop on my way out." He held up his lidded cup of cappuccino, which was actually very good.

"Leaving so soon?" The thought seemed to brighten her mood.

"No. I'll be here for about a month. I'm just on my way to Asheville for the afternoon."

She started to back away. "Don't let me keep you."

"You're not." He gestured to the chair on the other side of the table, and she stared at him, her lovely light gray eyes narrowed slightly, before she pulled it out and sat. "So, you own this store."

"Yes," she said slowly, as if it might be a trick question. "As I mentioned last night. And undoubtedly how you found me this morning."

He took his eyes off her for a moment to look around. He'd counted two other sporting goods stores on National Street, but Willa seemed to have found something that set hers apart, specializing in organic wear and environmentally friendly equipment, with a café in the store that made the place smell like roasting coffee beans, sharp and dark. "You must do a lot of hiking and camping."

"No. The last time I was in Cataract was during a field trip in third grade. I got poison ivy."

"Then you must love coffee."

"No more than usual." Willa nodded to the girl clerk. "That's my friend Rachel's territory."

He was confused. "Then why do you own a sporting goods store and café?"

She shrugged. "A few years ago I met someone who wanted to sell this place, and I needed something to do."

"And this is what you chose."

"Yes."

He leaned forward and put his elbows on the table. Why did this bother him so much? When he'd recognized her yesterday on Jackson Hill, sitting on top of her Jeep, he'd felt a surge of true happiness, like seeing a mentor. It was Willa Jackson, perpetrator of pranks so epic that on the rare occasion when he got together with his old classmates, it was still one of the first things they talked about. The care and detail and time that went into some of them was amazing—like her last one, pulling the fire alarm and then, when all the students were outside, unrolling a giant banner from the roof of the school, on which was written WILLA JACKSON IS THE WALLS OF WATER HIGH SCHOOL JOKER. "I watched you that day the police took you from the school, and you didn't look embarrassed. You looked relieved. As if, finally, you could stop pretending. I thought you were going to leave here and never look back."

She gave him an exasperated look. He didn't blame her. He should just shut up. This was none of his business.

No, there was one more thing he needed to say. "You're the reason I decided to follow my own path instead of coming back here and doing what everyone wanted me to do," he said, which made her brows rise. "No one thought you were capable of all that mayhem, and you showed them not to underestimate you. If you could be that brave, then I thought I could be, too. I owe that to you. To the Joker."

She shook her head. "That bravery, as you call it, resulted in a class-two misdemeanor when I pulled that fire alarm. I was charged, nearly expelled, and wasn't allowed to go to graduation. And my dad was fired because of me, because I took his keys and his computer passwords to pull my pranks. Don't glamorize it, Colin. I'm glad you found your path, and I'm happy it had something to do with me. But I found my path, too, even if it wasn't what you expected."

She thought her dad was fired? Colin knew for a fact that he'd quit. Colin had been there when it had happened. Why wouldn't her father have told her?

Willa took advantage of his silence and stood. "I have to get to work," she said. "Thanks for returning the invitation last night."

"Still not going?" he asked as he, too, stood.

"No. And before you ask again, I'm not planning some big prank."

"Too bad. That group could use some shaking up."

She avoided his eyes and walked past him. "I'm not the girl to do it."

He watched her walk away. She carried the scent of something fresh and sweet with her, like lemons. "Do you want to go out sometime?" he found himself calling after her, because somehow he knew he would regret it if he didn't.

She stopped abruptly. The girl clerk looked up from the café counter with a smile. Willa turned and walked back to him. "I don't think that's a good idea," she said in a low voice.

"I asked if you wanted to, not if it was a good idea."

"You think they're two different things?"

"With you, Willa, I think they are *definitely* two different things," he said, taking a sip of his cappuccino, not taking his eyes off her.

"You're only going to be here one month. I think it's high-handed, not to mention completely ridiculous, to think you can make me see the error of my ways in that short period of time." She had good instincts. She knew exactly what he was trying to do.

"Is that a challenge?"

"*No.*"

He walked to the door with a smile. "I'll be seeing you, Willa."

"Not if I see you first, Colin."

Oh, yes, that was definitely a challenge.

Ha. The old Willa was somewhere in there, after all.

"Where were you last night? Mama had a hissy fit," Paxton said when Colin got home that evening. She was coming in from work at the outreach center, where she had an office and oversaw the Osgood family's charity ventures. They just happened to meet in the driveway at the same time, a synchronicity they'd always had, a twin thing that he sometimes missed.

"Sorry," he said, putting his arm around Paxton as they walked inside. "I didn't mean to worry everyone. I fell asleep on someone's couch."

"Someone? How very unspecific," Paxton said as

they walked to the kitchen. The housekeeper, Nola, was making dinner. Nola had been a fixture at Hickory Cottage for years. Her family had worked there for generations. She was a stickler for manners and respect, and Paxton and Colin had always given it to her. In return she'd given them secret snacks. Colin stopped to forage around in the refrigerator. Nola tsked at him and gave him one of the rolls she'd just made, then shooed them both out.

Colin followed Paxton to the patio, where she stopped and turned to him. "Out with it. Whose couch did you fall asleep on?"

He took a bite of the roll and smiled at her, which used to result in a smile back. Not now.

When he'd set eyes on his sister in the foyer yesterday, it had been the first time in almost a year, when she'd flown up to spend a week with him in New York to celebrate their thirtieth birthday. She'd been so excited by the prospect of finally moving out of Hickory Cottage. But those plans had fallen through—something that had their mother's fingerprints all over it—and the difference between when he'd last seen Paxton and now was astounding. Unhappiness radiated from her like heat. She was beautiful, and always carried herself well, but she'd stayed too long in this house with their parents, shouldering absolutely everything it meant to be an Osgood. And it was partly his fault. He'd left her alone to deal with this. He'd known what was expected of him, and so had Paxton. But she'd embraced it. He'd wanted to establish something that was his alone, to prove that he could actually exist beyond

Walls of Water. To Paxton, *nothing* existed outside Walls of Water.

"Come on," Paxton said. "Tell me. Please?"

He finally shrugged and said, "It was Willa Jackson's couch."

Paxton looked surprised. "I had no idea you were friends with Willa."

"I'm not," he said, finishing the roll in another two bites. "When I was out yesterday, I saw her drop something, but I couldn't catch up with her, so I thought I'd just drop it by her house. I had no idea how tired I really was. I think I embarrassed her."

That made Paxton laugh. She didn't do that often enough.

"So tell me about Willa," he said, crossing his arms over his chest and leaning against the concrete balustrade.

Paxton adjusted that ever-present tote bag on her shoulder. "What do you want to know?"

"She seems to have a very quiet life."

"Yes." Paxton tilted her head. "Why are you surprised? Her family has always been quiet."

"But Willa was the Walls of Water High School Joker," he said.

"Yes?"

Paxton didn't get it. Neither did he, exactly. "I just thought she'd be more . . . outgoing."

"She grew up, Colin. We all did."

He scratched his hand against the side of his face. "Why doesn't she want to go to the gala? Her grandmother helped found the Women's Society Club."

"I don't know. When I sent her the invitation, I wrote her a personal note about wanting to include her grandmother. But she blew me off."

"She didn't want to have anything to do with the restoration?"

Paxton looked confused by the question. "I didn't ask her."

"You didn't ask if she had old photos or old papers? If she wanted to see what was going on inside as it was being restored? Anything?"

"There were enough photos on record to go by. Colin, honestly, this restoration was about contractors and designers and scouring art auctions and estate sales for period pieces. It didn't have anything to do with Willa. What could she have contributed?"

He shrugged as he looked out over the patio, to the pool, the pool house, and the mountain landscape beyond. The rolling mountains looked like kids playing under a big green blanket. He had to admit, there was nowhere in the world like this place. Part of his heart was still here, somewhere. He just wished he knew where so he could take it back. "I guess it just would have been a nice thing to do."

"I did the best I could," she snapped. "And where were you when all this was happening? You coordinated everything with the landscaping by phone and email. You wouldn't even do *that* in person."

"I didn't know you wanted me here for the duration." He paused, frowning at her reaction. "No one asked you to take on this project alone, Pax." He'd been surprised by Paxton's call last year, asking him to do the landscaping, but he couldn't say no. She'd wanted a large tree on the property, and after a lot of networking, Colin had found one being threatened by development nearby. But transplanting a tree that heavy and old had to be carefully choreographed. Everything had to be planned, down to the smallest detail. All year he'd been in touch weekly with the arborists they'd hired. And he'd taken off a month to oversee everything up until the grand opening of the Madam, which he'd considered a great sacrifice, because he hadn't been home for that long in over a decade.

Paxton threw her hands in the air. "The Blue Ridge Madam is the first thing anyone sees as they drive into town. It was an eyesore. It was either tear it down or restore it. That house is part of our town history. I did a good thing, even if I didn't ask Willa Jackson to help."

"Calm down, Pax. What's wrong?"

She closed her eyes and sighed. "Nothing's wrong. I just can't ever seem to do enough."

"Enough for who? Mom and Dad? You have to get over that. You're never going to be happy until you live your own life."

"Family is important, Colin. But that's not something I'd expect you to understand." She turned to leave. "Cover for me at dinner tonight, will you? Tell Mama and Daddy that I had to go finish up some work at the outreach center."

"Why?"

She spun back around and said, "Can't you do that for me? It's not as if you've been around for the past ten years to do it."

She was right. "Is that where you're really going?" he asked as she stepped back into the kitchen.

"No."

⁓

Paxton drove to Sebastian's house and pulled in front. His car wasn't there. That's when she remembered that he kept late hours on Thursdays at his office, which was the reason he'd had the time to go with her to visit her grandmother that morning. Now she had to see him *twice* in order to get through the day? She wondered how she survived before he came to town. Basically, she'd kept her stress to herself, sublimating it with red licorice or trying to work it out through her endless series of private lists.

She buzzed down the windows in her car and cut the engine. She felt better just sitting here, looking at Shade Tree Cottage. Reaching over to her tote bag, she brought out a small notebook, one of dozens she carried around. Sometimes she used whatever she had on hand, a paper napkin or the back of an envelope. It all ended up in her bag. Most of her lists were about control, about breaking down her life into manageable pieces. But some of the lists were simply wishes. There was nothing more satisfying than putting what you wanted most onto paper. It gave substance to something that was before as thin as air. It made it one step closer to being real.

She flipped to a clean sheet of paper and started a list about Sebastian. She had a lot of lists about him.

Sebastian's Favorite Things. If Sebastian and I Went on Vacation Together, Where Would We Go?

Today she started:

REASONS WHY SEBASTIAN MAKES ME FEEL BETTER

He doesn't care that I'm as tall as he is.
He doesn't care that I weigh more.
He holds my hand through things and doesn't think
    less of me for it.
He smells fantastic.
He's all clean lines and perfect manners.

"Do you do this often when I'm not here? Sit outside my house and work on your lists?"

Paxton gave a start and turned to see Sebastian, his hands on top of her car as he leaned down to look in her window. The sun on his skin highlighted how clear and poreless it was, and turned his blue eyes crystalline. She hadn't heard him approach, but she could see now that his car was parked behind hers in the driveway.

She smiled and quickly tucked her notebook away. "No, I was just waiting for you."

He opened the car door for her and helped her out. "It's too hot to be sitting in your car. Your hair is wet." He put his cool hand to the base of her bare neck, which made her want to shiver. It was a base reaction from a place deep within her, a well full of sharp longings and pipe dreams. She couldn't fill that well, couldn't stopper it, as hard as she tried. But for the sake of their friendship, she did everything she could not to show it.

She smiled. "You never sweat. Are you actually human?"

"I enjoy air-conditioning too much to ever be long without it. Come in." They walked to his door, where he unlocked it and gestured for her to enter first. He put his keys on the entryway table. She caught a glimpse of herself in the gold starburst mirror and immediately set her tote bag down and used both hands to slick back her hair, tucking all the loose strands into the knot she'd tied that morning.

"Have you had dinner yet?" he asked.

She dropped her hands. "No."

"Join me, then. I'll grill salmon. I'm glad I came home first."

"First?"

"Sometimes I go to that diner on the highway."

"The Happy Daze Diner?" she asked, disbelieving. The place seemed so unlike him. It had been a family diner at one time, now it was a hole-in-the-wall greasy spoon, still doing business because elderly people who remembered it in its heyday continued to frequent the place.

He smiled at her reaction. "Believe it or not, I have fond memories of the place. My great-aunt used to take me there when I was a kid." He loosened his tie. "So, how was your day?"

"The same. Until I got home this evening." Paxton hesitated. "I think my brother is interested in Willa Jackson."

He raised a single brow. "And you don't approve?" His tie hissed as he pulled it off. Maybe it was because

she was already on edge, but she thought it was a seductive sound. It made her skin prickle.

"No, it's not that. I'd love her forever if she made him
stay."

"Then what's the problem?" he asked.

She hesitated, still bothered by it. "He seems to
think I should have invited her to participate in the
restoration of the Blue Ridge Madam."

"Why didn't you?"

"It didn't occur to me," she said. "Do you think I
should have?"

He shrugged. "It would have been a nice thing to
do."

"That's what Colin said. I didn't mean to slight her."

"I know you didn't. You like being in control. It never
occurs to you to ask for help." He smiled and put a
hand to her cheek. "But some things are worth asking
for, darling."

"Easy for you to say," she said miserably.

"No, actually, it's not," he responded. "I'm going to
change. You haven't seen the upstairs since I redecorated my bedroom, have you?"

"No."

"Come on, then."

She knew where all the rooms were—the guest
room, the room with expensive exercise equipment in
it, the empty room he said he had vague plans to turn
into an office, and his master suite. He'd mentioned
having his bedroom painted last month, but she wasn't
prepared for the major overhaul he'd done. The gray
walls had a metallic sheen, and the furniture was all

black lacquer now. He'd spent most of his time when he first moved back decorating the downstairs and ridding the house of medieval décor left behind by the previous owner. She'd loved watching the transformation, watching it become more like Sebastian. This, though, wasn't anything like what she thought it would be. Dark, moody, stark, masculine.

She started to leave so he could change, but he told her to stay, and disappeared into his dressing room.

"Why did you choose a house this big, when there's only you?" she called as she walked around his bedroom. His bed was king-sized. There was room for someone else there; he just seemed to have no interest in issuing any invitations, though there was plenty of interest, from men and women alike.

"Every life needs a little space. It leaves room for good things to enter it."

"Wow, Sebastian. Profound."

She heard him laugh.

She walked by his bed, trailing her fingers along the silken black cover. She stopped to look at a painting over his bureau. She'd never seen it before. It was cracked and dark, obviously old. It looked like something that should be in a folk art museum. It was of a red bowl filled with ripe red berries. A black-and-yellow bird was perched on the edge of the bowl, looking out angrily, as if daring someone to take a berry from him. The tip of his beak was red from berry juice, or maybe blood. It was a little disturbing.

"That belonged to my great-aunt," Sebastian said. She could feel his chest brush the back of her arm as he came to a stop behind her. "She loved it. It hung in her living room, next to her woodstove. It's all I have by way of family heirlooms. I had it packed away for years."

"Why didn't you bring it out before now?" she asked, still staring at the painting.

"I wasn't sure I was going to stay."

"In this house?"

"No, in Walls of Water. I didn't know if things would work out." He paused. "But they did."

Her scalp tightened, as though she was in a barely avoided collision. She hadn't known she'd almost lost him. What was so wrong with this place that people wanted to leave it? What was so wrong with home and history and family, even if they got on your nerves? Her back still to him, she said, "You've mentioned your great-aunt twice tonight. I don't think you've ever talked about her before."

"She was the only person in my family I knew loved me without reservation. But she passed away when I was ten."

Sebastian didn't talk much about his family, but from what little he had told her, she knew his father was verbally abusive, and that he had a much older brother who now lived in West Virginia. They had lived in a trailer park on the west side of town, near the county line. She guessed she'd answered her own question. Maybe there were some things you simply had to get away from. She could understand it from Sebastian. She still didn't understand it from her brother. To change the subject, she smiled and turned around and said, "Dinner?"

She didn't realize how close he was. "Unless there's something else you want to do up here," he said.

She wouldn't touch that. She couldn't. "Are you implying I need to use your workout room?" she joked.

He lowered his eyes and turned away. "Never, darling. I love you just the way you are."

FIVE

Unearthed

It was hard to believe on a day like today, when Willa and Rachel were so busy their lunch consisted of only filched cappuccino doughnuts and iced coffee from the café, but business on National Street actually fell off sharply after Thanksgiving. They could go days in the gray winter, sometimes an entire week, without a single customer. There was always a slight upswing in February, the town's coldest month, when out-of-towners liked to hike into the national park to see the famous waterfalls when they froze, like bridal veils, against the mountains. But mostly, from December to April, those who made their living off tourists just suffered through, dreaming of warmer months, of kingfisher-blue skies and leaves so green they looked like they'd just been painted, as if the color would smear if you touched it.

It was those slow months leading into spring when many transplants got restless and decided to leave. Willa had seen it happen time and time again. Rachel had lasted here more than a year, but Willa could see how hard the cold months were on someone as hyper as she was. Willa was dreading this coming winter. She was afraid she was going to lose Rachel to it. And Rachel and her coffee and chocolate were the only things making life here bearable, the only things she really looked forward to now that the restoration of the Madam was almost complete and she didn't have an ex-cuse to drive up Jackson Hill every day to see how it was going.

"Willa, look," Rachel said at about four o'clock that afternoon, when they finally had a quiet moment in the store. Willa turned to see that Rachel had stopped re-stocking the snack case at the coffee bar, and was look-ing out the window. "Tall, dark, and rich is heading this way."

Willa looked up to see Colin Osgood walking by the store window, heading for the door.

"Oh, crap. Tell him I'm not here," she said, and turned to the storeroom behind the counter.

"What is the matter with you?" Rachel called after her.

Willa disappeared, closing the door behind her, just as she heard the store bell ring.

What was the matter with her? That was a good question. But it was hard to explain, especially to some-one like Rachel. The winters were tough on Willa, too—maybe even more so, because she knew she couldn't leave. That was the big difference between Willa and Rachel, between Willa and all the other transplants. Her grandmother was here. Her father's house was here. Her history was here. Sometimes she would lean against the front counter, chin in hand, and stare at the snow, craving something else, something different from life, which made her feel that nervous pull in her stomach, like how she would feel when weeks would go by in school after she'd promised herself she wouldn't do anything stupid again. The feeling would just get worse and worse, until she found herself hanging a rope of leotards out the dance tower window at two in the morning, just so everyone coming to school would think that a group of dancers had gotten stuck up there and had to tie their clothes together and climb out naked.

That's why she wanted to stay far, far away from Colin Osgood. No one, *no one*, had ever said that she'd inspired them before. No one had ever said they'd admired her for what she'd done. It went against everything she'd been told, everything anyone who had ever suffered through high school wanted to believe, that if you just tried hard enough, you could actually get away from who you used to be. But not for the first time, she found herself wondering: What if who she was then was her truer self?

She heard voices out in the store. The timbre of Colin's low voice, Rachel's laughter.

Then, suddenly, the knob to the storeroom was turning. Her back was to the door, so she instinctively pushed against it. But he had the advantage of more strength and momentum, and it was a losing battle. She gave up and stepped out of the way, letting the door fling open.

Colin reached out and caught the door before it hit the wall, then looked at her strangely. It had been a long day, and her hair felt about two feet thick, so at one point she'd taken a bandana from stock and used it to push her hair away from her face. Completing today's lovely ensemble were jeans, platform sneakers, and a T-shirt that read: *Go Au Naturel! Au Naturel Sporting Goods and Café, Walls of Water, North Carolina*. It, of course, had a coffee stain on it. "Why were you leaning against the door?" he asked.

"I told you you wouldn't see me if I saw you first."

"I didn't think that meant you would literally hide from me."

"Not one of my finer moments," she admitted.

He was wearing khakis and loafers. His aviators were tucked into the collar of his light blue T-shirt. He looked so put-together and in control of himself. This was apparently the unique power of all Osgoods—their ability to make her feel slightly out of control.

"What do you want, Colin?"

"I want you to come up to the Madam with me," he said. "There's something I want to show you."

Okay, that got her attention, but then, he probably assumed that it would. "I can't. I'm working," she said. To prove her point, she picked up a box of paper cups and inched past him through the doorway.

"It won't take long," he said, following her across the store to the coffee bar. "We found something on the property today, and maybe you can help us figure out who it belonged to."

"I doubt it. I don't know anything about that house," she said. And it was true, unfortunately. Her grandmother had never talked about her life there. She handed the cups to Rachel, who was giving her a very juvenile you're-talking-to-a-boy look. She turned around and found Colin closer than she'd expected. "What did you find?"

He leaned forward, tall and easy, and smiled down on her. "Come with me and find out," he said seductively. He smelled intriguing, different from the sandalwood and patchouli she was used to—the National Street set was notoriously bohemian. Colin's scent was sharp and fresh, both foreign and oddly familiar. Green, expensive.

She took a step back. "I can't."

"Are you saying you're not curious at all?"

"Oh, she's curious," Rachel said.

Willa cut her eyes at her.

"Then come with me," Colin said. "It won't take long."

It was too much to resist. She'd been wanting to see it for over a year, and now she had the perfect excuse, one that didn't involve evening dresses, small talk, or Paxton Osgood. It did, however, involve Colin Osgood, his confusing motives, and some definite sexual tension. But he would be leaving in a month, so it wasn't as if she would have to hide from him forever. "Rachel, hold down the fort," she said. "I'll be right back."

"Take your time," Rachel said with a knowing smile.

"I'm forming some theories about cappuccino with one raw sugar."

Yes, Willa just bet she was.

"She remembered my order," Colin said as he stepped ahead of Willa and opened the door for her.

"She does that. I'll follow you in my Jeep," she said as she started to turn to where she'd parked farther down the sidewalk.

He grabbed her elbow. "That's okay. I'll drive us." He pointed to the big black Mercedes in front of them. He clicked the key fob he was holding, and the lights flashed and the doors unlocked. She recognized this car. It was hard to miss. It belonged to his father.

He stepped off the curb and opened the car door for her. She sighed, deciding that arguing would only take more time, and got in. She was almost swallowed by the huge leather seats. Once Colin got behind the big wheel—there was something seriously overcompensating about this car—he put on his aviators and backed out. He smoothly maneuvered the car through the traffic on National Street, one hand on the steering wheel, the other on his knee.

After several minutes of silence, she turned to him and said, "Why are you going to be here a whole month?"

The side of his mouth lifted at her insinuation that it felt like forever. "I took some time off to help Paxton with the Madam. And to attend the gala."

"Where do you live now?"

"New York is my home base. But I travel a lot."

Just then they turned the corner to the steep driveway up to the Madam, and she stopped trying to make small talk. She'd never been beyond this point. She turned her attention away from Colin and watched the house as it got closer. Giddiness felt like her skin, her whole self, was stretching into a smile. *This is going to be something significant,* she thought. *No ghosts. This is going to feel like coming home.*

When he stopped the car in the luggage drop-off lane in front of the house, she couldn't wait to get out. Something was off, though. She couldn't quite put her finger on it. The wind blew in a sharp gust past her, sounding like voices in her ears. She turned in the direction of the wind and whispers. At the edge of the plateau, there was a backhoe at work and a few men in hard hats were standing around.

"The tree is gone," she said, realizing what was missing.

Colin walked around to her side of the car. "The peach tree, yes."

"It was a peach tree?" That surprised her. "I didn't realize peach trees could grow at this elevation."

"They can grow, they just can't bear fruit. The springs are too cold here. Kills the buds." He leaned against the car beside her.

"Then why plant a peach tree here?"

He shrugged. "Your guess is as good as mine. Paxton said it wasn't in any of the old photos of the place, so it had to have come up after your family moved out. Since it's not historical, and not fruit-bearing, she decided it could go."

"How did you know it was a peach tree if it's never

borne fruit? I don't think anyone knew it was a peach tree."

"I'm a landscape architect," he said.

It was all starting to make sense. "Ah. You're doing the landscaping. That's why you're here."

"Yes. I drew up the plans, then contracted the work out before I arrived. My biggest contribution was finding a live oak to put on the property. I found a one-hundred-and-fifty-year-old one over in Buncombe County. It was being threatened by development, and the developer didn't want to get into it with the environmentalists, so he agreed to split the cost with us in order to transplant it here. It's been almost a year in the making, getting the tree ready. The highway is going to have to close on Tuesday just to move it here." He turned to her and smiled. "You should come watch."

"Come watch you plant a tree? Gee, you know how to show a girl a good time."

That made him laugh. "It's a lot more than that. Trust me. How can you own a sporting goods store and not like nature?"

Before she could answer, one of the men at the dig site suddenly yelled, "Hey, Stick Man!"

Colin turned his head but otherwise didn't move from his relaxed position, leaning against the car. She could feel a ripple of tension go through him, though. In what she knew with absolute certainty was a deliberate maneuver, he stared at the man who had called to him, until it became clear he wasn't going to yell back.

The man sighed and walked from the dig site over to the car. As he got closer, Willa recognized him as Dave

Jeffries. They had all gone to high school together. He'd been on the football team, and was still thick in the chest, though less from muscle these days. "What's up, Dave?" Colin asked as soon as Dave stopped in front of him.

"Just after you left, we dug up something else." He held up a heavy rusted cast-iron frying pan, still crusted with dirt.

Colin took it from him and studied it. "A frying pan?"

"Yep."

"This just gets more interesting."

Dave smiled when he saw Willa. "Willa Jackson," he said, pushing his hard hat back. "I almost never see you around. Remember that time you programmed the period bell to ring every five minutes? That was great. We kept filing out into the hallway every five minutes, and the teachers kept trying to get us back into the classrooms." He gave her an assessing look, then wagged his finger between her and Colin. "You and the Stick Man aren't together, are you? Because you could give ol' Dave a try if you're lonely."

"Tempting offer, Dave," Willa said. "But no thanks."

Dave laughed and punched Colin on the arm with what seemed like entirely too much force. But what did she know? Maybe it was a man thing. "Good luck," he said to Colin.

As soon as he walked away, Willa turned to Colin and said, "Stick Man?"

"That's what they used to call me in high school. Thanks to Dave."

"Because you're so tall?"

"That's what everyone thought."

She waited, then said, "You're not going to tell me?"

He sighed. "Dave called me Stick Man because he said I acted like I had a stick up my ass."

Willa was so surprised that she laughed without meaning to. She put her hand to her mouth and said, "Sorry."

"Well, to be fair, it was true. I was a little rigid. It was how the men I knew acted, so I thought I was supposed to act that way, too. Guys like Dave loved to make fun of guys like me, guys who seemed to have no concept of fun. I can't tell you how great it felt our senior year when everyone thought I was the Joker. They looked at me and thought, *Wow, I didn't know he had that in him.*"

"I remember that feeling," she said. Then, before they could get into another discussion about bravery, or her apparent lack of it now, she asked, "So, what did you want to show me here?"

He took off his sunglasses and hooked them on the collar of his shirt, then motioned for her to follow him up the steps to the front portico of the house. The place was huge, much larger than she'd imagined from a distance. It overwhelmed her. She'd spent so much time watching this place from a distance that it felt faintly surreal to actually be climbing the steps, to actually touch the columns.

"While digging up the stump of the peach tree today, we found some buried treasure. A suitcase and a fedora. And apparently a frying pan," he added, giving the rusty thing a spin in his hand. "When they showed me the fedora, it gave me chills, because every kid who has broken into the Madam for the past forty years has claimed to see a floating fedora in the house. My grandmother used to scare us by telling us stories of the ghost who lived here."

"Did you ever see it?" she asked.

"I kept my eyes closed the one time I broke in here with my friends," he said. "And I will deny that if you ever tell another person."

She gave him an odd look. Who would she tell?

"What about you?" he asked. "Did you ever see it?"

"I never broke in," she said.

"Are you kidding me? All the stunts you pulled, and you never once broke into the Madam?"

"I've never been this close to it before." She actually reached out and touched the side of the house, as if to make sure it was real.

"Why not?"

She let her hand drop, afraid that she looked silly. "For the same reason everyone else broke in. Ghosts. My grandmother told me those stories, too."

"*You're* afraid of ghosts?" he asked.

"I just think things that are laid to rest should stay there," she said, realizing she sounded a lot like her grandmother. She stepped over to the suitcase sitting on the edge of the portico. It was made of black leather that was rotting and covered in dirt, but it was still surprisingly intact. The contents of the suitcase had been removed and were lined up neatly beside it, next to the fedora.

She crouched down and looked through everything,

though she wasn't sure why. It wasn't as if she'd recognize anything from the time her grandmother lived here. Her grandmother's life, as far as Georgie was concerned, started after she left this place.

The suitcase items were mostly dated men's clothing in cotton and linen. But there was also a disintegrating newspaper and an open scrapbook. She carefully lifted the pages of the scrapbook and looked through it. It was bulging with clippings, its pages yellow and brittle with glue. Whoever this belonged to liked to follow what movie stars were doing in the 1930s. That seemed to be the purpose of the book. But every so often there were real photos. They were very old, of blurry people in an orchard of some sort.

"Do these trees in the background look like the peach tree that was planted here?" she asked, and Colin looked over her shoulder. He was considerably closer to her than she thought he needed to be, and there was no doubt in her mind that he was doing it on purpose.

"Yes, they do. Interesting clue."

As she looked through the rest of the book, she found a high school diploma from Upton Orphan School for Boys in Upton, Texas, made out to someone named Tucker Devlin.

"Does any of this seem familiar?" Colin asked from behind her, where he was still arcing over her like a wave.

"Not really, just . . ." She stopped when she reached the last page. There was a single photo of a handsome man in a light suit, wearing a fedora, maybe the same fedora buried with the suitcase. He looked like he knew he was beautiful. He looked like he could get anything he wanted.

"What?" Colin asked.

"I don't know. There's something familiar about him." Willa closed the scrapbook, not able to figure it out.

"That Asheville newspaper in the suitcase dates this back to August 1936, the year your family moved out," Colin said as he stepped back.

"That was the month and year the Women's Society Club formed, according to the invitations your sister sent," Willa added as she stood. "I don't know anything about this. Sorry. Some of my grandmother's things are stored in my attic. Maybe there's a clue to this Tucker Devlin person. I could look."

"That would be great." He smiled. "Would you like to see the inside of the house?"

It took everything she had not to shout, *Yes, please!*

He went to the huge eight-panel door with the hand-blown bull's-eye glass on either side of it. There was a brass plaque to the left that read THE HISTORIC BLUE RIDGE MADAM INN. The door looked like it would be heavy, but it clicked open easily.

Her hands were actually shaking as she stepped inside to a cool blast from the past. The first thing she saw was the grand staircase hugging the wall in a long, curving slope. At the top of the staircase was a portrait of a woman with dark hair and gray eyes, wearing a stunning dark blue gown. She looked down on the lobby with a wistful expression.

It was overwhelming to think her grandmother had lived here like this. It was a hard thing to reconcile, the grandmother she knew and the one who had once flitted through these rooms, these lovely, opulent rooms. She wanted so desperately to feel connected to this place, to feel . . . something. But as she looked around, she couldn't feel a thing.

Not a single thing.

The foyer had been turned into a lobby, and there was a dark cherry check-in desk to the side. A woman in jeans and a T-shirt was on the phone. When she saw Colin, she gave him a wave.

Colin waved back as he led Willa to the right, through an archway and into the dining room. Dozens of round tables filled the space, which was awash in light from the ceiling-high windows. There was a large wainscoted fireplace along one wall, flanked by period sitting chairs. "Paxton said she found a chef with five-star credentials. The Rebecca Restaurant will be open to the public, but apparently they're booked into next year."

"Why Rebecca?" she asked.

"That was the name of your great-great-grandfather's wife. He built the Madam for her."

"Oh," she said, embarrassed that she didn't know.

He led her out of the dining room and directly across the lobby to the opposite archway. "This was the original library," Colin said. "Now it's a sitting room. There will be afternoon tea served here for the guests."

It, like most of the downstairs, was covered in dark paneling. There was a twin fireplace to the one in the restaurant, but flanking it were shelves full of old books. Ornately upholstered couches and chairs were scattered around.

The woman who'd been on the phone entered at that moment. "Sorry about that, Colin. It's always something. I'm still trying to find a laundry service. Paxton threw me a curveball when she asked if the Madam might be ready for overnight guests the night of the gala."

Colin made the introductions. "Willa, this is Maria, the manager. Paxton stole her away from the Grand Devereaux Inn in Charleston. She's the best in the business. Maria, you're looking at a direct Blue Ridge Madam descendant. This is Willa Jackson. Her ancestors built this place."

"This is an honor," Maria said. "Welcome, Willa."

"Thank you," Willa said. She was beginning to feel supremely uncomfortable, and heat was creeping up her neck. She didn't belong here. Certainly, intellectually, she'd always known that. The house hadn't been in her family for decades. That was why she'd stayed away. But she'd always harbored the hope, leftover from childhood, that somehow, magically, one day someone would realize that they'd got it all wrong and this was really all hers.

"Maria can back me up," Colin said. "You've seen the fedora, haven't you?"

Maria laughed. "I'm sure it was my imagination.

Once you hear a place might be haunted, every creak becomes a ghost."

"I'm going to show Willa around upstairs," Colin said. "Are the guest rooms still unlocked?"

"Yes," Maria said. "Enjoy."

They walked back into the foyer. "Beyond the check-in desk is the banquet hall. That's where the Women's Society Club will be holding the gala," Colin said as he and Willa walked up the stairs. Once they reached the top, Colin stopped at the portrait of the lady in blue. "That's your great-great-grandmother, Rebecca Jackson. The painting was found wrapped in blankets in a closet. It's a miracle it survived all the years of looting."

Willa stared at her. So this was her grandmother's grandmother. Did Grandmother Georgie know her? She had no idea. "I have her eyes," she found herself saying.

"I know."

"This is the first time I've ever seen her."

Colin shook his head. "Paxton should have let you in on all of this. I don't know why she didn't."

"I wouldn't have been much help," Willa said. "She did a great job on her own."

"The guest rooms are this way."

She stopped him from turning the corner. "No. I've seen enough."

"What's wrong?"

"Nothing. It's a gorgeous place. Thanks for the tour, but I really have to get back. Sorry I couldn't be more help with the buried treasure." She thought she was past all of this. She had no idea why it was affecting her this way.

She started to turn. And that's when the earth moved.

She paused, then met Colin's dark eyes. He looked as confused as she was.

"Did you feel that?" she asked.

"Yes," he said seriously. "And I don't like it."

"That's not . . . the ghost, is it?"

He took a moment to smile at her, as if she'd said something cute.

Then he took off down the staircase. She followed him outside, only to feel that the shaking was more pronounced out in the open. The ground was rumbling, making the large outdoor chandelier sway.

Colin looked over to where they were digging up the roots of the peach tree, which had created a fairly significant hole. "If I didn't know better, I'd say it feels like they hit a gas line. But there aren't any gas lines here. And we had all the other underground utilities marked."

The rumbling seemed to be getting louder, vibrating the air around them in waves that made Willa's eardrums pound.

"Whatever it is, it's going to blow. Get inside with Maria," Colin said as he ran to the edge of the portico, waving his arms, trying to get the attention of the men at the dig site. "Get back," he yelled. "Get back now!"

The men looked at him and didn't hesitate. They ran with full force away from the hole.

Colin turned as the rumbling escalated. Willa hadn't

gone inside. She was still standing there, one hand against the wall now to keep her balance. He surprised her by grabbing her and flattening her against the side of the house. Several seconds passed, the rumbling escalating until she was sure something was going to happen. Something was going to explode. Crack. Fall away. Come to light. She squeezed her eyes shut and buried her face in Colin's chest, her hands fisted in his shirt. But just as it reached its crescendo, the rumbling abruptly stopped and everything became eerily quiet, with the exception of the chandelier slowly creaking as it swayed.

Colin pulled back, and he and Willa looked at each other for one long, heated moment. Then they simultaneously turned toward the backhoe. A cluster of black-and-yellow birds had settled on the machinery and were looking into the hole. One of the men cautiously approached. When he looked in, the expression on his face registered complete shock.

"What is it?" Colin called.

He tipped his hard hat back. "You're gonna want to see this for yourself."

"Are you okay?" Colin asked, turning back to Willa. He cupped the side of her head with one palm.

Willa nodded as she slowly loosened her hold on his shirt. Colin stepped back, then jumped off the portico and walked toward the hole. After a few deep breaths, Willa followed.

Colin got there first and looked in. *"Jesus Christ."*

"What is it?" she asked.

"I think we just found the owner of the suitcase," Colin said.

Willa looked in the hole. It took a moment to realize that what she thought was a large stone wasn't a stone at all.

It was a human skull.

SIX

The Fairy Tale

Paxton broke through the surface of the water and swam laps until her arms burned. Her pace was frenetic, as though she was trying to swim away from something and if she just pushed a little more, she would be free of it. When she couldn't push herself anymore, she floated for a while. It was dark, but the pool lights were so bright that she couldn't see the stars. She wanted to stay like this forever, the water shutting out all sounds, disconnected from everything.

She finally stood, because this was no solution, and her mother would be coming out soon to tell her she'd spent too much time in the water, anyway. She pushed her wet hair out of her face and let her hands rest on top of her head as she took a deep breath and told herself that she could fix this. She could fix anything if she just put her mind to it.

She didn't know when exactly she realized someone was outside with her. It was a gradual awareness, like the way you slowly wake up to the sound of rain at night. She turned in the water to see Sebastian sitting on one of the lounge chairs. He'd taken off his suit jacket and had tossed it onto the lounge chair next to him. He was watching her with a hooded expression. If there was one thing she had learned about him, it was that he kept his emotions close to the vest. If he didn't want her to know how he felt, he gave absolutely nothing away.

"Sebastian. What are you doing here?" He'd never been to her house before. She pushed through the water to the steps and got out, grabbing the towel she'd put by the edge of the pool. She dried off while walking to him, feeling self-conscious because he'd never seen her in a bathing suit before. Not that it mattered. Not to him, anyway.

He stood as she approached, picking up his suit jacket and tossing it over his shoulder. "I heard about the skeleton found at the Blue Ridge Madam today. I wanted to see if you were all right. You wouldn't answer your phone."

"It's fine. Everything will be fine," she said, which was what she'd been saying all afternoon. If she said it enough, maybe it would even become true.

"But how are *you*?"

"I'm fine, too." She wrapped her towel tightly around

her, holding it together at her chest with her hand. She looked back at the main house, wondering what her mother thought of Sebastian being here. "I can't believe you braved my parents just to see if I was all right. I hope they were nice to you."

He didn't answer directly. "I'm used to the looks. I've gotten them all my life. The important thing is, your mother let me in. That wouldn't have happened fifteen years ago. Don't worry about me. I can survive just about anything."

For some reason, that struck a nerve. She had no idea why. "You don't think I can?"

He stared at her without a word. She'd never really been on her own. She was still living with her parents. She understood why he might think that.

"Let's go in," she said, leading him to the pool house. She looked back to the main house one more time. Her mother was now watching from the French doors. "How long have you been out here?"

"Awhile. You have a nice backstroke."

Paxton opened the door, and he followed her in. She quickly grabbed some notes she'd been making from the coffee table and stuffed them in her tote bag.

"Would you like something to drink? I think all I have is whiskey." Her mother had stocked the liquor cabinet in the pool house when she'd redecorated last year, but whiskey was the only thing left, because Paxton didn't like it. She found herself thinking she should restock. Sebastian always had a full bar. But restocking meant going into Hickory Cottage and facing her mother's inevitable insinuations that she might be drinking too much. Never mind that Paxton rarely drank and that it had taken an entire year to go through what little had been in her liquor cabinet in the first place.

"No, thank you," he said as he looked around. Her mother had had the place redecorated as a crazy dysfunctional thank-you to Paxton for not moving out entirely. The place was meant to feel like a vacation home or a beach house. The colors were white and sand and gold, all the furniture was square and soft, and the carpet was textured. They weren't choices Paxton would have made. Nothing in this place bore her signature, not like at Sebastian's house. Whenever she dreamed of being in a home, it was never here. Sometimes it was the townhouse she'd almost bought last year. Sometimes it was a place she'd never seen before. But she always knew it was hers. This place smelled of lemons. Always. And she could never make it go away. The home she dreamed of smelled of fresh grass and doughnuts.

"So, you're fine," Sebastian said as he sat down on her couch. He wasn't interested in the details of the skeleton they'd found at the Madam. He was worried about *her*. No one else around her had reacted like this to the news.

"Yes," she said, trying to laugh. "Of course."

He didn't look like he believed her. Sometimes she didn't think it was fair that he knew her this well.

"Well, actually," she said, "I feel like hyperventilating."

"Do you want to sit down?"

"No. Because I can't hyperventilate. I want to, but I can't. It's all built up here, and I can't let it out." She patted her chest with the hand holding the towel together. "Colin is going crazy trying to form a backup plan, because that one-hundred-and-fifty-year-old oak tree is scheduled to be delivered on Tuesday, and it will have to be planted right away or we'll lose it. Not to mention the several hundred thousand dollars it's taken to uproot it and bring it here. But we don't know if the police will clear the scene and let us plant it yet. And do you want to know why I turned off my phone?" She didn't wait for him to answer. "Because the Women's Society Club members keep calling, worried about being able to hold the gala at the Madam now. Several members wanted to have the gala at the country club, anyway, but they were outvoted. They've already called the club, scrambling to get it for the night of the gala, like they wanted to in the first place. They seem so eager to believe that this is going to make everything, all the hard work that went into the restoration, fail. The manager at the Madam even said some people have called, worried about their reservations, when it doesn't even officially open for guests until *September*." Her voice was pitching, and she stopped and took a deep breath.

Sebastian stood and walked over to her. He took her by her arms, looked calmly into her eyes, and said, "You can't control everything, Pax. I keep trying to tell you this. You have this remarkable *resistance* against letting some things just happen. If you take a step back, you'll see that when this blows over, no one will question having the gala at the Madam. Right now everyone is drinking bad wine made of sour grapes and hysteria. Let them drink it, and let them regret it in the morning. And for every person who cancels their reservation, someone will reserve a room solely because of this. There are a lot of people out there who like a taste of the macabre."

"But this isn't meant to be macabre!" she said. "This is supposed to be perfect."

"Nothing is ever perfect. No matter how much you'd like for it to appear that way."

She shook her head. She knew that. She just didn't know how to live any other way. She'd been this way her entire life, crying if her ponytails were uneven or if she wasn't the best in dance class. She didn't know how to stop it, as much as she wanted to.

"Just let it go, darling," he said, drawing his arms around her, not caring that she was wet. This, *this*, was why she loved him so much. "Whatever it takes, just let it go." With her hand still clutching the towel, she couldn't hug him back and stay covered, but she realized she liked that she could fold herself into him this way. She liked feeling small. She put her head on his shoulder and could feel his breath on her neck.

Her heart picked up speed, and she was sure he could hear it.

As the seconds passed by, she could almost feel the rope winding around them as the sheer force of her desperation and desire pulled her closer to him. She slowly let the towel drop and lifted her arms around him, grazing her chest with his. She raised her head from his shoulder and put her cheek to his, nuzzling him slightly, just a small graze. She could feel his beard stubble, but his hair was so light she'd failed to notice it before.

She was overwhelmed. That's the only reason she could think to justify her actions, her *weakness*. She turned her head in an excruciatingly slow movement, and her lips found his. Her hands went to his hair, and she opened her lips. He wasn't unwilling. That's what surprised her the most. After a moment of surprise, he actually began to kiss her back. Her heart *sang*. Before she knew it, she was walking him to the couch and pushing him to sit. She straddled him, trying to kiss past the rest of his barriers, to get him into that seductive place when their eyes had met all those years ago when he was kissing someone else. If she just tried hard enough, she could make this happen. She could make him love her the way she loved him.

"Paxton . . ." Sebastian finally said in between her kisses. "Think this through. Is this really a good idea?"

She opened her eyes and slowly leaned back. They were both breathing heavily. His color was high, and it made him even more beautiful, that rose-red flush along his cheeks. His hands were tight on her buttocks.

What was she doing? He'd told her to let it go, but she was sure he hadn't meant this way. And yet he was going to *let* her. Oh, God. How pitiful could she get?

She pulled away quickly, and found the towel and wrapped it around her again.

He leaned forward and put his elbows on his knees. He stayed that way, bowed over, clasping his hands in

front of him, his breath still quick from their encounter. He was staring at the floor, seeming to collect
his thoughts.

He finally stood. "I think I should go," he said.

She tried to smile as she nodded that she understood.

Without another word, he left.

She wanted to move out but didn't want to disappoint her parents. She wanted help with everything she
had to do but was too proud to ask. The Blue Ridge
Madam project was supposed to cement their family's
reputation, but there was a skeleton casting a pall over
the project now. The Women's Society Club's seventy-
fifth anniversary gala was supposed to be the crowning
achievement of her presidency, but it was being threatened with a last-minute change of venue. And she'd
wanted so badly for Sebastian to be something he
wasn't, that just now, in a matter of minutes, she may
very well have ruined the best thing that had ever happened to her.

How could someone with a life this full feel this
empty?

She went to the liquor cabinet and took out the vile
bottle of whiskey and poured a glass. With a deep
breath and a grimace, she forced it down.

Trying to stay awake after a very long day, Willa let the
humid night air blow on her as she drove home from
Rachel's party. She hadn't intended to go to Rachel's
regular Friday-night cookout. In fact, she usually said

no. Friday night was vacuuming night. Sometimes jogging night, if she felt like it or had eaten one too many cookies at the store. Wild and crazy stuff. But the sight of that skull at the Blue Ridge Madam earlier that day made her want to be around people that night. Colin had taken her back to her store after the discovery of the skeleton, and then he'd rushed back to the Madam with an apology. She hadn't heard from him since.

She'd left the store with Rachel and had gone straight to Rachel's house. That had been seven hours ago. She'd stayed too late. Too late for her, anyway. The cookout party was still going strong when she'd left. Rachel wasn't your typical twenty-two-year-old, except when she got around other twenty-two-year-olds, and that was when Willa realized how much difference eight years can make in a life. She didn't exactly miss being that age—she'd been a college dropout and drank too much and partied too hard—but she did miss that sense of living in the moment, of living only to *feel*.

After she'd said her goodbyes, she'd headed back down the long road leading into Walls of Water. Rachel and her boyfriend rented a tiny farmhouse near the county line. A few miles into her drive, she passed a convenience store called Gas Me Up, a place frequented by college students in the summer because it sold cheap beer and didn't always ask for ID. The parking lot had a few cars in it and, as Willa yawned, she assumed her eyes were playing tricks on her when she thought she recognized one of them.

No, surely not.

She slowed down to make sure.

Yes, that was definitely Paxton Osgood's white BMW roadster.

And that was definitely Paxton coming out of the store.

What on earth was *she* doing there? She didn't think Paxton knew what this side of midnight looked like, much less this side of town.

Willa had slowed down so much that the car behind her honked. She pulled over to the side of the road, and the car zoomed past.

That's when she saw their old classmate Robbie Roberts come out of the store behind Paxton.

He'd grown up to be handsome in a fading kind of way. He was cocky and could be charming when he wanted to be. But he got drunk too often, worked only long enough to collect unemployment, and was reputedly thrown out of the house by his wife on a weekly basis.

Robbie was trouble, but he was soft trouble. A lover, not a fighter.

But his two friends, the men hanging around outside the store, were definitely hard trouble.

Of all the things Willa thought she knew about Paxton Osgood, she'd been most certain that Paxton could handle herself in any situation. Paxton didn't need anyone to protect her. She had an air about her that made people pay attention. She had a way of speaking that made people listen. And it didn't hurt that in heels, she was probably six feet tall. She wasn't a person someone would take on lightly or easily.

But as Willa watched what was happening, she realized that Paxton was, probably for the first time in her
life, completely out of her element. It was nearly one in
the morning at an all-night convenience store on a side
of town that didn't often see the likes of her, in her red
sundress and strappy heels with bright red roses on
them. She was standing outside of the doors now,
stopped there by the men, her arms heavy with bags
that looked like they contained bottles of wine and
potato chips. Cheap wine and chips? Not her usual
fare. Her hair, normally in a chignon as tight as a baby's
fist, was only half up. The other half was falling around
her pretty, wide face. She seemed strangely unfocused
and uneasy on her feet.

She was *drunk*.

Willa would have thought it was funny, would have
enjoyed watching the drunken spectacle of someone
who had made a lifetime commitment to perfection,
whose simple existence made all the women around
her feel less somehow, fall flat on her face . . . if it
weren't for the men surrounding her.

There was a strange but universal understanding
among women. On some level, all women knew, they all
understood, the fear of being outnumbered, of being
helpless. It throbbed in their chests when they thought
about the times they left stores and were followed. The
knocks on their car windows as they were sitting alone
at red lights, and strangers asking for rides. Having too
much to drink and losing their ability to be forceful
enough to just say no. Smiling at strange men coming
on to them, not wanting to hurt their feelings, not want-

ing to make a scene. All women remembered these things, even if they had never happened to them personally. It was a part of their collective unconscious.

Willa couldn't just sit there on the side of the road and not help. She had to do something. What, she wasn't quite sure. But she jerked her Jeep in gear anyway, and crossed the road to the convenience store's parking lot, thinking that nothing about this day had been normal, nothing had been boring.

And she would never, ever admit, not even to herself, that she kind of liked it.

She stopped in front of the group, the Jeep's high beams on. She saw Paxton jerk her arm away from one of the men trying to touch her, then walk forward, only to be blocked by the other man.

Willa reached into her bag for her pepper spray and opened the door.

"Hi, Paxton," she said. Her heart was racing, and she could feel the adrenaline surge. "What are you doing here?"

The men turned to her. Paxton's head jerked up, and Willa saw it, her fear, primal. She was the weak animal surrounded by predators. *Help me.*

"Look, a mini one. We got enough for a real party now," the man holding Paxton's arm said. He had abuse written all over him. It had happened to him. He had delivered it. It was so much a part of his psyche that he couldn't look at another person and not imagine what they would look like with bruises. Willa felt it, the way he looked at her neck and the thin skin along her cheekbones.

"Why don't you let go of her? I'm pretty sure she wants to leave," Willa said. Her hand was already throbbing from clenching the can of pepper spray. She was hyperaware of everything around her, every small sound, every change in the air.

Robbie snickered. He'd always been the boy to hang out with the rough bunch at school, not really one of them but close enough. And like most people, he'd figured close enough was better than not fitting in at all. "Come on, Willa, how often do we get a drunk prom queen around here? And she sent me a love letter in high school. She denied it and made everyone laugh at me, but she sent it to me. Admit it, Paxton."

"Robbie, for God's sake, I sent you that letter," Willa said. "I was the Joker. That's the kind of stupid thing I did back then. She didn't have anything to do with it."

He gave her a confused look.

Willa left them and marched to the convenience store's door and called inside, "Call 911."

The clerk looked up from his magazine, then looked back down, ignoring her.

"That's my brother," the second man said. "He ain't calling no one."

Willa slowly backed up. She knew she could run to her Jeep and call 911 and wait with her doors locked. But that would leave Paxton to fend for herself, and the last thing any woman wanted in this kind of situation was to look around and see all the people who could help her doing nothing. Paxton seemed to know what she was thinking. She was trying to meet her eyes, trying to keep Willa from looking away. *Don't leave me.*

"Paxton, set down your bags," Willa finally said.

"But . . ."

"Just do it. Let's take a ride in my Jeep, okay?"

"I have my car."

"I know. But let's go in my Jeep." She made a small gesture with her hand, and Paxton's eyes went to the can of pepper spray. Paxton dropped her bags to the concrete. The wine bottles smashed.

"She ain't going nowhere," the man holding her arm said. "Except maybe behind the building for a little fun."

Willa took a deep breath, then lifted the can and aimed. This was her last course of action, but she didn't hesitate. Plus, she'd spray-painted enough things in her misspent youth to have pretty good aim. She got the first man in the face. The second man moved, and she had to chase him to the door before she got him. Once she did, she lunged over and grabbed Paxton's arm, dropping her spray in the process.

They were almost to the Jeep when Robbie stepped in front of them. The first man was coughing and rubbing his eyes, making it worse, making his anger rise. He yelled at Robbie to grab the bitches. The second man had run into the store to get the clerk, who was now coming toward the doors. Willa didn't have anything to defend them with now.

"Was the letter really a Joker prank?" he asked.

"*Yes,*" Willa said.

"Oh. Sorry, Paxton."

Paxton was holding on to Willa now with a force that was going to leave marks.

Robbie dropped to his knees and covered his face, screaming as if he, too, had been maced. Willa had no idea what he was doing until he took a break from his theatrics to say, "Go, goddamnit."

And that's exactly what they did.

Willa jumped behind the wheel, and Paxton fell into the passenger seat. Willa was trembling so much she had trouble putting the Jeep in reverse. After she had set up particularly big pranks at school, which had sometimes taken all night, she remembered crawling back into bed and shaking like this. It hadn't felt bad, more like a thaw. When she finally got the Jeep in gear, Paxton nearly fell out from the speed with which Willa backed out of the parking lot. She had to grab a handful of Paxton's dress to keep her inside.

Once they were on the road, a long stretch that ran parallel to the highway, Paxton was finally able to sit upright. The wind from the open top of the Jeep made their hair fly, and the only sound was the flapping of their clothing, like sheets on a line. Willa kept checking her rearview mirror, relaxing only when a couple of miles had passed and she realized they weren't being followed.

Neither of them said anything for a very long time.

Finally, Paxton asked, "Do you have any tissues?"

Willa turned to her. Tears were streaming down her cheeks, and her nose was running. "I have some paper napkins in the glove compartment."

Paxton fumbled around until she found the napkins. "I'm not crying," she said.

"Okay."

"No, really, I'm not. I got hit by some of the pepper spray."

"Oh," Willa said. "Sorry about that. I thought my aim was better."

Paxton snorted, which made Willa smile.

"Where are we going?" Paxton asked, blowing her nose as they reached the town proper.

"To your house."

That had an immediate reaction. "No, don't take me home!" Paxton said loudly. "Let me out right now." She started fumbling with the door handle.

Willa had to pull over because she was afraid Paxton was going to try to leap out of the Jeep while it was still moving. Now that the adrenaline rush was over, she could finally see what a problem she had. She had drunk Paxton Osgood in her car, and she had absolutely no idea what to do with her. "Where do you want me to take you, then?" she asked. They were in front of a Tudor-style house in Paxton's neighborhood. A dog barked from somewhere inside. "Kirsty Lemon's?"

Paxton leaned her head back against the seat. "God, no. She'd love this."

"I thought you two were friends."

"Whatever that means," Paxton said, which surprised Willa. Society ladies always seemed so hand-in-glove, giving looks to one another that only they could interpret, sharing secrets.

"Sebastian's?"

Paxton seemed to think about that. She finally said softly, "No."

That left only one place. Great. Willa put the Jeep in gear and made a U-turn. "What were you doing at the Gas Me Up at this hour, anyway?" she said as she drove.

"It was the only place I could get alcohol at this time of night and no one would see me," Paxton said as she rubbed her eyes. "God, that spray was strong, and I only got a little bit of it. I hope they feel it for days."

"No one in their right mind goes there after dark, not even college kids."

"Well, I didn't know that," Paxton said defensively. "It's the first time I've been there."

"Why tonight?"

"Because my life is crap and I needed alcohol."

Paxton Osgood's life was crap. Right. "You didn't have any alcohol in your house?"

"I drank it all," she said.

"In a house the size of Hickory Cottage?"

"I drank all the liquor in *my* house. The pool house. And there was no way I could go to my parents' house for more. My mother would've given me hell. She always gives me hell. You know who else gives me hell? The Women's Society Club. One skeleton found at the Madam, and suddenly they think the whole project is a wash. As if they don't have tons of skeletons in their closets. If you only knew." Paxton turned in her seat and Willa could feel her staring at her. "And you gave me hell, too. In high school."

"Only once," Willa pointed out.

"I can't believe it was you who wrote that note to Robbie Roberts."

"I'm sorry." Willa pulled to the curb and cut the engine. "I really am."

"I remember when I saw that note. You copied my handwriting so well I thought at first I *had* written it. You could've gone into forgery."

Willa climbed out and said, "Yes, that would have made my dad very proud."

Paxton looked around, finally realizing they'd come to a stop. "Where are we?"

"This is my house. Come on."

"You're going to let me stay at your house?"

"The Ritz is too far to drive to."

Paxton wasn't steady on her feet, so Willa held her elbow and led her up the steps. She unlocked the door and led Paxton to the couch, then left the room and returned with a pillow and a blanket.

Paxton took off her shoes and propped the pillow up on the couch. "This is a great couch."

"I'm thinking of calling it the Osgood Memorial Couch. Your brother slept on it, too." Willa left again, this time to the kitchen, where she wet a dishcloth with cold water. She brought it out and handed it to Paxton.

"My brother likes you, you know," Paxton said, lying back and putting the cool cloth over her swollen eyes. "Make him stay."

Willa flipped out the blanket and covered Paxton. "I'm not involved with your brother."

"You will be. You know why? Because that's what's supposed to happen. That's the fairy tale. You meet, you fall in love, you kiss, and *neither of you is revolted by it.* You get married and have kids and live happily ever after."

"The not-being-revolted part is a nice touch," Willa said.

"It comes from experience. I'm in love with Sebastian Rogers. But he's not in love with me."

Willa probably should have been surprised, but she wasn't. She locked the door and turned out the light. When things went dark, she stood there for a moment. "Your life isn't nearly as glamorous as I thought it was," she said into the darkness.

"What tipped you off? The drunk run to the Gas Me Up, or admitting that I'm in love with a man who might be gay?"

Despite her tone, Willa got the feeling this was more serious than Paxton was letting on. "It's a tie," Willa said, which made Paxton laugh a little. She was too used to people judging her, Willa realized.

Then something Willa never thought would happen suddenly did.

She actually felt sorry for Paxton Osgood.

This was enough revelation for one night. Exhausted, Willa left the living room and headed upstairs to her bedroom.

"Thank you, Willa," Paxton called after her.

"You're welcome, Paxton."

SEVEN

Relativity

Paxton slowly opened her eyes, which took effort. Her lashes seemed to be glued together.

She sat up on her elbows, a small movement that actually felt like being slammed against a wall. She groaned but powered through it and sat all the way up.

She looked around. She was in a small house filled with dated furniture, except for the insanely soft gray couch she was lying on. She was facing a picture window, and there was a black-and-yellow bird sitting on the sill, staring inside. She stared back at it, confused and strangely mesmerized. A shrill ringing sound suddenly made her jump and, startled by her movements, the bird flew off.

She put her hands to her head. Good God, what was that noise?

She heard footsteps and turned to see Willa Jackson stumble into the room wearing cotton shorts and a tank top, both twisted from sleep. Her short hair was poofy, like a cloud around her face.

Paxton had often thought that all Willa needed was a white muslin nightgown, a big bow in her hair, and a porcelain doll clutched to her chest, and she would look exactly like one of those pale-eyed, intense children in very old photos. Paxton had never felt very comfortable around her.

"I thought I turned off your phone last night when it wouldn't stop ringing. Is it possessed?" Willa said, lunging for Paxton's cellphone, which Paxton just now realized was on the end table beside her.

Willa flipped open the phone and said, "Hello?" She paused. "I'm Willa. Who are you?" Willa's hand, which had been over her eyes as if to block out the light from the window, suddenly dropped. "Oh." She handed the phone to Paxton. "It's for you."

Paxton took it, trying not to make any sudden movements for fear her head might fall off. "Of course it's for me. It's my phone."

Willa frowned and turned and left the room. Someone wasn't a morning person.

"Hello?" Paxton said into the phone.

"I'm in the pool house, and you're not. Where are you?" It was Colin.

She looked around. "I'm not sure. I think I'm at Willa Jackson's house."

"That would explain her answering your phone. What are you doing there?" Colin asked.

It was all coming back to her. And she wasn't about to share it with him, with anyone. God, if it got out what a *fool* she'd made of herself . . .

"Have you been there all night?"

"I think so," she said.

Colin paused, and she could tell what conclusions he was coming to. "Are you drunk? There's an empty whiskey bottle in your living room."

"No, not anymore. And get out of my house."

He laughed. "What happened?"

"Like I'm going to tell you."

"You know I'm going to find out sooner or later."

"Over my dead body," she snarled.

"Okay, all right. Listen, the reason I called is because I don't seem to have much authority when it comes to the Blue Ridge Madam. People want to talk to *you*, not me. Meet me at the police station. I need some answers about clearing the scene in order to move that tree, and I need them now."

"Right," she said, trying to rally. "Give me an hour."

She hung up, then sat there, her head cradled in her hands. Even her hair hurt. She didn't know how much time had passed before Willa came back and said, "Are you all right?"

She looked up at her. She was holding a cup of coffee and a bottle of Advil. She handed both to Paxton. "You saved me last night," Paxton said. She'd never forget the glare of the lights of the Jeep as it came to a stop, then the sight of Willa getting out and coming to her rescue. She'd never been so glad to see anyone in her entire life.

Willa shrugged. "You were out of your element."

"I can't believe you did that for me. Why?"

Willa looked like she thought it was an odd question. "When someone needs help, you help. Right? I thought that was a tenet of the Women's Society Club . . . your 'sparkling good deeds,'" she said, quoting what Paxton had put on the invitations to the gala.

Paxton wasn't sure what bothered her most, that Willa saw her as a charity case or that she could never imagine any of her friends in the club coming to her rescue like that. The Women's Society Club was about helping people in the most distant way possible, about giving money and then dressing up and celebrating it. The Osgood family charity trust that Paxton ran did real work, and didn't ask to be congratulated. So why on earth did she still continue with the club? History, she supposed. Legacy. That was important to her.

She swallowed a few tablets with the strong coffee, then set the coffee and bottle of Advil on the coffee table in front of her and felt the contents churn in her stomach. "Thank you. For everything. I've got to go. Where is my tote bag?" She suddenly panicked. "Where is my *car*?"

There was a knock at the door. "I don't know where your tote bag is, but your car is still at the Gas Me Up. Don't worry, I've taken care of it," Willa said as she went to the door and opened it.

It was, of all people, Sebastian. He took one look at Willa in her little sleep outfit and said, "My God, there's a woman under those jeans and T-shirts, after all."

Willa rolled her eyes but smiled.

The morning light was hitting his pale hair, making him seem angelic. He should have been a welcome sight, but he was the last person she wanted to see right now. Paxton stood to turn away but immediately regretted the move. Her head felt full and tight, which made her slightly nauseated. "What is he doing here?" she asked Willa.

Willa closed the door behind Sebastian, and the light left him, making him human again. "He kept calling your cellphone last night. I had to get up and answer it. He was worried about you. I told him you were fine and sleeping over here."

Sebastian walked up to Paxton and pushed some of her loose hair out of her eyes. He managed to bring everything that had happened between them last night back to her with just one look. All she wanted. All he couldn't give. "She forgot to mention that, at some point, a substantial amount of alcohol was obviously involved," he said. "Darling, if your eyes were any more red, you'd have X-ray vision."

Paxton stepped back, avoiding his eyes now. "I'm fine. It's just the pepper spray."

"The *what*?"

Paxton looked to Willa, who shook her head. She hadn't told him. "Nothing."

Sebastian gave her an assessing look. "I told Willa I'd come get you and take you to your car this morning, but I'm not sure you're able to drive."

"Of course I am," she said. "I'm fine, really. Don't worry about me. I just need to use the bathroom first."

"It's through the kitchen, at the back of the house." Willa pointed, and Paxton gratefully stumbled in that direction. She walked through the pretty yellow kitchen and found the half-bath. She closed the door and put her hands on the sink, taking deep breaths so she wouldn't get sick. She couldn't believe Sebastian saw her like this, pitiful and hungover, obviously drowning herself in her sorrows, as if she couldn't handle her stresses any better, as if she couldn't handle his rejection.

Why had Willa let him come over? She remembered telling Willa that she was in love with him, the *one* thing she'd sworn she'd never say out loud. She should have known. Secrets always find a way out.

She splashed her face with cold water and managed to scrub the mascara from around her eyes. She'd put mascara on? She looked down at herself. And a red dress and heels. All this to go to a convenience store for wine. What had she been thinking? That was the point, she guessed. She hadn't been thinking. She pinned her hair back and sighed. It wasn't much help. She decided to get this over with, and walked back to the living room.

Sebastian and Willa were talking easily. They both went quiet when she entered the room, the proverbial pink elephant.

Sebastian turned. "Shall we?"

"Yes, I know you want to get to that free clinic you have this weekend," Paxton said as she walked to the door. "Thanks again, Willa."

"Sure," Willa said. "Anytime."

Once they were outside, Sebastian opened the door to his Audi, and Paxton slid in. He got behind the wheel and pulled out of the neighborhood in silence.

"Do you want to talk about what happened last night?" he finally asked.

"No."

"I know you don't want to talk about what happened between us," he said quietly. "I was referring to what happened with you and Willa."

"It's just between us girls," Paxton said, staring out the side window. She smiled weakly. "Well, I guess you are one of the girls."

"I'm not a girl, Paxton," he said, and the coolness in his voice made her turn to him.

"I didn't mean to imply you were. Not literally. I just meant—"

"Where is your car?" he interrupted her by asking.

"The Gas Me Up on State Boulevard."

"What is it doing there? Did it break down?"

"No."

"Then what were you doing there?"

She turned back to the window. "It doesn't matter."

Sebastian pulled into the lot of the Gas Me Up, and the place was busy with early-morning commuters making pit stops. He parked beside her BMW, which was, mercifully, intact. She'd had no idea how she was going to explain it to Sebastian or her family if those cretins had trashed her car in revenge.

"You don't happen to have any Visine on you, do you?" she asked. "My mother is going to hate seeing me like this."

"I have some at home," he said. "Do you want me to take you there?"

"No thanks." She was thirty years old. She shouldn't have to sneak back home after a night out. "This would be a lot easier if I didn't have to go home and change."

"Bring some clothes to keep in my house. If you need them, they'll be there." She turned to him, surprised by the intimacy of the offer, especially after last night. "Why didn't you call me, Pax?" he asked, and she realized, incredibly, that he was hurt. "If you didn't want to go home, you could have stayed with me."

"Willa offered to drop me off at your house, but I told her not to," she said.

"Why?"

"Because I was drunk. And we both know that me out of control isn't a pretty sight."

"I always think you're beautiful."

She couldn't handle this. Not now. She opened the door. "I'll see you soon. Thank you for the ride."

He reached out and took her hand, not letting her get out. "I want to help you, Pax."

"I know you do. That's why I'm not asking again."

❧

When Paxton got back to Hickory Cottage, she grabbed her tote bag, which she had obviously left in her car and had been so relieved to find, and entered the house as quietly as possible. Her mother was a late sleeper, her father an early riser in golfing weather. There was a good chance she could just slip through and not be seen.

Once Paxton got to the kitchen, she thought she was home free. She smiled at Nola, a square older woman with red hair fading to gray, and so many freckles that she looked like she'd been splattered with a paintbrush. She was kneading dough on the kitchen island. Plumes of flour were floating around her, making her look like she was in a snow globe.

Paxton's smile slowly faded when she realized there was someone else in the kitchen.

"Mama!" Paxton said. "What are you doing up this early?"

Sophia was sitting at the kitchen table with a cup of tea in front of her. She was in her long white eyelet nightgown and robe, her hair pushed back with a wide headband. She slept in her diamond stud earrings every night. Even if she hadn't worn them that day, she actually put them on to go to bed.

"I heard you leave last night," Sophia said.

"Yes," Paxton said. "I couldn't sleep."

"Do you want to tell me where you've been?" Sophia asked. "Were you with that Sebastian person? I couldn't believe it when he just dropped by last night. I . . . I don't know how to act around him." She tugged at the lapels of her robe.

"No, Mama. I wasn't with Sebastian last night."

"Well, I don't want you coming in at these hours, especially when there's so much going on right now with the Madam. Where is your head? Honestly, Paxton, what's gotten into you?"

"I don't know," she answered.

Paxton and her mother had had a good relationship

throughout Paxton's childhood, mainly because Paxton felt there had been no other choice. Her mother had been fanatical about planning special bonding times. When Paxton was a teenager, her friends had even envied her relationship with her mother. Everyone knew that neither Paxton nor Sophia scheduled anything on Sunday afternoons, because that was popcorn-and-pedicures time, when mother and daughter sat in the family room and watched sappy movies and tried out beauty products. And Paxton could remember her mother carrying dresses she'd ordered into her bedroom, almost invisible behind tiers of taffeta, as they'd planned for formal dances. She'd loved helping Paxton pick out what to wear. And her mother had exquisite taste. Paxton could still remember dresses her mother wore more than twenty-five years ago. Imprinted in her memory were shiny blue ones, sparkly white ones, wispy rose-colored ones. She remembered watching her mother and father dance at charity functions and parties. From a very young age, she knew she wanted that for herself, not the dresses—though she'd thought for a while that was all it took—but the dream of dancing with the man you love, having him hold you like he never wanted to let you go.

It was only this past year that things with her mother had gotten tense, and she was beginning to understand why. She and her mother had never had an adult relationship. And getting to one was like trying to walk in thick mud, one excruciating step at a time.

Paxton inched her way toward the French doors. "If you'll excuse me, I've got to change and leave again.

Colin called me this morning. I'm going to meet him at the police station to see what we can do about getting the scene cleared at the Madam for the tree planting."

That made Sophia smile. "Colin and his trees."

It made Paxton smile, too. Colin had always had a thing about trees. He'd spent half his childhood in the hickory grove on the estate, just lying there and staring up at the branches, as if the history of the world could be found there.

Sophia's smile suddenly faded. "Just because he stayed out all night when he first got back doesn't mean you get to do it, too."

It was a double standard Paxton was used to by now. Sophia had focused all her efforts on shaping Paxton into who she wanted her to be, but she had only a peripheral effect on Colin, whom everyone had assumed was being molded by their father in some mysterious man way on the golf course. But Colin had broken away from whatever ephemeral expectations their father had, and by then it was too late for Sophia to rope him back in.

Sophia stood, then sighed. She looked around the kitchen in a drowsy, languid kind of way. "I'm going to lie down until breakfast. Nola, wake me if I fall asleep."

Nola and Paxton watched Sophia leave, like something out of an old movie. "Will you be staying for breakfast?" Nola asked when Sophia had made her exit.

Paxton swallowed. "No. I don't think I could handle food right now."

Nola smiled as Paxton walked out. "It's about time," she said.

For reasons she didn't understand, and her grand-mother probably would have said were signs, Osgoods were crawling out of the woodwork and into Willa's perfectly normal life, upsetting the balance.

But thankfully, Willa figured she wasn't going to see much of either Colin or Paxton anymore, what with the brouhaha going on up at the Madam.

Over the weekend, a news crew from Asheville had come to do a story on the skeleton found at the Blue Ridge Madam, then reported that the unconfirmed cause of death could possibly have been homicide, because someone had noticed trauma to the skull. The news crew had also been given the name Tucker Devlin from an unnamed source, someone who had obviously seen the scrapbook and the high school diploma, and they had found a man by the same name who had a record in Asheville for swindling several people out of their money in January 1936. He'd been a traveling salesman.

A traveling salesman? A possible murder? That had tongues wagging, and Willa was as curious as the next person, in a distant kind of way. What went on at the Madam didn't have anything to do with her, and probably never would. The ghosts up there were none of her business.

Or so she thought until the police came to see her on Sunday.

"Did you see that man?" Rachel called from the coffee bar after their last customer left on Sunday afternoon. Willa had just cashed out the store register and looked up to see Rachel writing in her coffee notebook. "He'd been hiking for a week, and he's finally going home today. You know what he ordered? An iced mocha latte. That's a drink for people who are ready for comfort. I'm telling you, it's a science." She finished writing and waved her coffee notebook at Willa.

Today Rachel's super-short hair was in spikes and she was wearing one of the waterproof tops the store sold, along with a tiny plaid skirt. The whole ensemble was so off-kilter, so Rachel, that it made Willa smile.

"What?" Rachel asked, when she saw Willa staring at her.

Willa shook her head, thinking how glad she was that Rachel had walked into her store a year and a half ago. "Nothing."

"Quick, tell me what kind of coffee you want right now."

"I don't want any coffee right now," Willa said.

"But if you did, what would it be?"

"I don't know. Something frozen and sweet. Chocolate and caramel."

"Ha!" Rachel said. "That means you were just thinking of something that makes you happy."

"Well, you've got me there. I was."

The bell over the door rang, and they both turned to see who it was.

But no one was there.

"That's the second time that's happened," Rachel said, frowning. "When are you going to fix that bell? That freaks me out."

"I thought you said you didn't believe in ghosts," Willa teased as she zipped the deposit bag and went to the storeroom to put it in the safe.

The bell rang again while she was in the storeroom.

"Willa?" Rachel called.

Willa walked out, saying, "Okay, I promise I'll fix it."

"Someone's here to see you."

She felt a little catch in her chest, because for some reason she thought it would be Colin coming to see her again. She didn't have much time to process why exactly that would make her happy, especially since she had convinced herself that he was nothing but trouble, because when she turned to the man standing at the door, she saw that it wasn't Colin. It was Woody Olsen, a detective from the Walls of Water Police Department.

Willa's father had taught Woody in high school, and Woody had always respected him. Woody had been the one who had called Willa in Nashville and told her about her father being hit and killed on the interstate. She'd been so young and directionless and full of grief at the time that Woody had helped her arrange everything, and had even given the eulogy at the funeral. She sent him a fruit basket every Christmas instead of ever saying thank you in person. She just couldn't bear it. Even now, she still stiffened upon sight of him, because she would forever associate him with being the bearer of bad news. It wasn't fair, but she couldn't help it. Her mind instantly went to what could have happened, what bad news he was bringing now.

"Hi, Willa," Woody said. His eyes were big and perpetually watery, which made it hard to tell if there was really anything wrong. "I need to ask you a few questions about your grandmother. Do you have a few minutes?"

"My grandmother?"

"Nothing's wrong. I promise." He smiled and gestured slowly to the café, as if the slower his movements, the calmer she would be. "Let's have a seat," he said.

Confused, Willa walked over to the café and sat. Woody took the chair opposite her. He was a skinny man but had a large belly. His tie sat on his stomach like a pet. "What's this all about, Woody?" she asked.

"Your grandmother isn't able communicate anymore, so as her only living relative, our questions have to come to you. That's all."

"But why do you have questions about her?"

Woody took a notepad from his interior jacket pocket. "When did your grandmother's family move out of the Blue Ridge Madam?"

"Nineteen thirty-six. I don't know the exact date." She shook her head. "Why?"

"Did she ever mention anything about anyone being buried at the Madam?"

This was about the skeleton. Her shoulders dropped with some relief. "Oh. That. No. She never talked about her time at the Madam. Sorry."

Woody looked at the pages of his notepad, not meeting her eyes. "I understand she was pregnant when her family lost the house."

Willa hesitated. "Yes."

"Did she ever say who the father was?"

"No. She was a teenager and unmarried, which was obviously scandalous at the time. She didn't like talking about it."

"Did your father know?"

"He might have. He always said it was private. I didn't ask a lot of questions back then. I should have." She bent her head, trying to meet Woody's eyes. "This is ridiculous, Woody. The man buried up there isn't the father of Georgie's child. There's no connection."

He finally looked up. "Colin Osgood told me you had a look at the things buried with the skeleton."

"Yes," she said. "I mean, this was before we knew there was a skeleton buried there. He asked me to look through the things to see if I recognized anything."

"So you looked at the scrapbook."

She stared at him blankly. "Yes."

"You didn't recognize anything?"

"No. Did you?"

Woody put the notepad back in his jacket. "Thanks for your time, Willa. That's all."

He got up to leave, and a terrible thought suddenly occurred to Willa. "Woody."

He turned as he got to the door.

"You don't think my grandmother had anything to do with that skeleton being buried up there, do you?"

He hesitated. "Whatever happened, it happened a long time ago. I doubt we'll ever know the whole story."

"That didn't answer my question."

"If anything else comes up, I'll let you know. Don't worry. It probably won't." He opened the door, then offered her a small smile. "Thanks for the fruit baskets. I always enjoy them."

Willa turned to Rachel, who had heard the whole thing.

"I need to . . ." Willa said as she stood. She couldn't seem to finish the sentence. She didn't know exactly what she needed to do.

Rachel nodded. "Go," she said.

Willa went directly to the nursing home, something she rarely did this late in the day, because her grandmother had a tendency to get restless at sundown. But her protective instincts took her there.

Georgie had already had her dinner and had been sedated, so Willa sat by her bed and tried to get her mind around what was going on. Willa knew that there was nothing in the items found in the grave that tied her grandmother to this Tucker Devlin person. She had no idea why Woody thought there was.

She remembered that the newspaper found in the suitcase was dated August 1936. She wished she knew when exactly her grandmother moved out. If it was before then, there would be nothing to worry about.

The whole thing was preposterous, of course. Her grandmother had always been a decent person, a beautiful bird of a woman who had known a lot of hardship, but who had an incredible work ethic and made a life for her and her beloved son. She would never hurt anyone.

Willa stood and kissed her grandmother's forehead, wishing there was some magical way to snap her fingers, like a hypnotist, and bring her grandmother back from whatever faraway place she had floated off to.

She went to the nurses' station and asked them to contact her if anyone came to see her grandmother. She didn't mention the police specifically, but it was who she was thinking of.

As she was talking to the nurse, she saw someone round the corner beyond the station. It was Paxton Osgood, obviously there to visit her own grandmother. She looked considerably better than the last time Willa had seen her. That is to say, she was back to looking perfect.

If Willa called out hello, she was fairly certain Paxton would act as if Friday night had never happened. And if she was going to pretend that Friday night never happened, then they had no connection, no reason to exchange pleasantries in the first place. So Willa was just going to turn around and leave.

But that's when something suddenly occurred to her. Agatha. Of course.

Willa had never had much contact with Agatha Osgood, but she'd spent enough time at the nursing home to have heard how loud and stubborn, and sometimes outright mean, she could be. But Agatha and Georgie had been good friends as girls. Once Georgie had given birth to her son, Agatha had even helped raise him for the first few years of his life while Georgie worked for the Osgood family. They'd actually all lived together at Hickory Cottage until Ham was six years old. That's when Agatha got married. Willa's father once said his mother didn't feel right living there after that. The two women soon grew apart, not for any specific reason, it seemed. But Willa's father had once said that Georgie hadn't thought of herself as one of their group anymore.

Willa followed Paxton down the far-right hallway and watched her disappear into a room. When Willa reached the room, she looked inside with surprise. Agatha's quarters were like a fine Southern lady's parlor. There were beautiful oil portraits on the wall, a matching suite of furniture, even a small refrigerator. It looked like, at any moment, a maid in a white uniform was going to enter and serve strawberry tea and petits fours.

Paxton was standing with her back to Willa. Willa cleared her throat and said from the doorway, "Paxton?"

Paxton turned and, after a moment of surprise, actually looked relieved. "Look, Nana," Paxton said. "You have company. Isn't that nice?"

Agatha was sitting on a love seat in front of her window, her body in a permanent stoop that reminded Willa of a seashell. But her movements were surprisingly quick, her head swinging around in the direction of Willa's voice in the doorway. "Who is it? Who is there?" she asked.

"It's Willa Jackson, Mrs. Osgood," Willa said.

Agatha immediately tried to stand. "What is it? Is something wrong with Georgie?"

"No, ma'am," Willa rushed to say. "She's asleep right now."

Agatha sat back in her seat. "Then what do you want?" she demanded.

Both Agatha and Paxton were staring at her. Willa was struck by how much alike those stares were. Paxton certainly favored her grandmother. "I was wondering if I could talk to you about my grandmother. I could come back later if this is a bad time."

"Of course it's not a bad time," Paxton said, waving for Willa to enter. "Wouldn't that be nice, Nana? To talk about the old days?"

"Stop being stupid, Paxton. It doesn't become you," Agatha said, then turned to Willa. "What do you want to know?"

Willa walked in a few steps. "I . . . It's hard to say. You were friends."

"We *are* friends," Agatha snapped. "She's still here. I'm still here. And as long as we are, we'll always be friends."

"You knew her the year her family moved out of the Madam?" Willa asked.

"Yes, of course I did. She moved in with me after that."

"Do you remember anyone dying at the Madam that year? And then being buried under the peach tree? The police were asking me questions about Grandmother Georgie this afternoon. They were insinuating she might have had something to do with it. That she had something to do with *him*, the man buried there. But that's preposterous. You knew her then. She would never have done anything like that." She caught Paxton's frantic hand motion a little too late. Uh-oh. This was obviously something they were trying to keep from Agatha.

The change in Agatha was remarkable. She actually gave a physical start and her eyes grew wide, looking like large brown marbles pressed into hard dirt. "What? What is this about? Paxton?"

"It's okay, Nana," Paxton said, walking over to her and patting her arm, which Agatha jerked away. "We took down the old tree at the Madam, and there was a skeleton buried there. Nothing to worry about. Everything's fine now. In fact, we're bringing in a nice big tree to replace it."

"The moment you told me that you'd bought the Madam, I knew this was coming. You found him," Agatha said. "You found Tucker Devlin."

Willa and Paxton exchanged glances. The mood in the room turned tense. A cool breeze floated eerily by, smelling of peaches.

"How did you know his name?" Paxton asked carefully.

"Anyone who met him would never forget his name."

Despite the fact that she knew Paxton was upset with her for bringing this up, Willa found herself taking another step forward. "You knew him?"

"He called himself a traveling salesman. He was really a con man. But even that didn't do him justice. He was . . . *magic*." Agatha whispered that last word, as if it had power. Without realizing it, Paxton and Willa moved in closer to each other, an action both would be hard-pressed to explain. "I'll never forget the day we first saw him. Georgie and I were sitting in the grass up at the Madam, making crowns out of clover flowers. The wind was high that day, and I remember our dresses were flapping around our legs. I kept losing my sight when my hair crossed my eyes, so Georgie laughed and made me turn so she could braid my hair, and that's when we saw him walking up the hill with his dusty suitcase. We had heard of him, of course. He'd been in town for a while selling ladies' cosmetics, and the older ladies kept him to themselves. But he was on to bigger and better things that day. He reached the door of the Madam and paused, then turned to us. When he saw what Georgie was doing, saw me holding my dress so it wouldn't fly up, he smiled—smiled like God looking down on His children. He whistled a few strange notes, and the wind *stopped*. Just like that." Agatha paused. "The man could whistle and make the wind stop."

When Willa's and Paxton's arms touched, they jerked apart and put some space between them.

"Don't worry, Willa. Your grandmother didn't kill him," Agatha said. "And I know that for sure."

Willa smiled. "Well, it's a relief to hear someone say that."

"Because *I* killed him," Agatha finished.

EIGHT

Party Girls

Paxton took swift and immediate action. "I think you've upset her enough," she said, ushering Willa to the door with the skill of a hostess herding her last guests out. "Now she's talking nonsense."

"I haven't talked nonsense a day in my life!" Agatha barked.

Once in the hallway, Paxton said, "She's delicate, and she doesn't know what she's talking about. Don't come back here and upset her. I mean it."

Paxton went back into the room and closed the door. Willa was tempted to get angry, but she'd seen something in Paxton that tempered the emotion. Paxton wanted to protect her grandmother. Just like Willa did.

So Willa left the nursing home with even more questions than she'd started with. There had been a surprising vehemence in her voice when Agatha had declared that her friendship to Georgie still existed, as if it was a living, breathing thing, something that came to life the moment it happened and didn't just go away because they no longer acknowledged it. How far would that friendship go? Far enough to lie? Or far enough to tell the truth?

She wondered if Paxton was thinking the same thing.

One thing she knew for sure: Willa was on her own when it came to finding answers now. She'd seen the wall go up. There was no way Paxton would let her talk to Agatha again.

When she got home, she changed clothes and climbed the stairs to the only other place she knew to look for clues.

The attic.

It had been a long time since she'd had any reason to come up here. It was dim and dusty, and spiderwebs wrapped around the entire area, making it look like a large ball of string. She broke through the webs to see boxes piled to the rafters. Her old toys from childhood. Her dad's teaching awards. Her grandmother's things were in large white boxes under some quilted packing blankets. Willa had been away at college when her dad had moved her grandmother into the house from her apartment, so Willa had no idea what was in those boxes. Probably a little bit of everything. Her dad never threw anything out. The couch Willa had finally gotten rid of last week had been the same couch her father and mother had bought when they'd first married. Over the years, it had been patched, re-stuffed and re-stitched, then finally covered with a blanket to hide the grape jelly and coffee stains.

She took a deep breath and began to unearth the boxes that had her grandmother's name on them. One at a time, she brought them downstairs, until they filled half of the living room.

She picked a box at random, sat down in front of it, then opened it.

She almost gave in to tears at the scent that whooshed out at her. Cedar and lavender, with undertones of borax and bleach. Scents she would always associate with her grandmother. Georgie had been obsessively neat, and Willa remembered her father telling her that walking into Georgie's apartment and finding dishes piled in her sink had been his first clue that something was wrong. Georgie never forgot to do the dishes. Her memory had only gotten worse after that.

Her father had packed these boxes, and it must have been hard for him. He always, stridently, respected his mother's privacy. That was probably why it looked like this box had been packed with his eyes closed.

The box contained items Willa remembered from Grandmother Georgie's sparse living room. She began to take things out. Everything was individually wrapped in newspaper. A crystal candy dish. Two embroidered pillows. A Bible. A photo album.

Ah. That had possibilities.

After she unwrapped it, she set the album on her lap and cracked it open. She remembered looking through

it as a child. It contained photos of her father. Only her
father. Grandmother Georgie had had some of Willa's
school photos framed and sitting on her television, but
her son had had a book of his own. Willa found herself
smiling as she flipped through the pages. There was
Ham as a baby, swallowed up in a large white christen-
ing gown. There he was as a chubby little boy in front
of what looked like Hickory Cottage. School pictures.
Graduation. Then came a series of photos of him in his
twenties, randy and carefree. Willa had always loved
these particular photos, watching her father's charm as
it grew around him. If she hadn't known exactly the
path his life had taken, the one where he'd ended up a
widowed, sedate chemistry teacher, she would have assumed from these photos that he was destined to become a charismatic public figure. A movie star. A
politician.

But he'd wanted a small life. He'd wanted the life his
mother had wanted him to have, because her opinion
meant that much to him.

She turned the page, and her smile faded. There was
her father, at about age thirty. He wouldn't marry for
another eight years. Willa wouldn't be born for more
than ten. He was wearing funny, dated pants, and his
hair was longer than she'd ever seen it. His hands were
in his pockets, and he was looking at the camera in a
way that almost made the photo tremble with the force
of his personality. He looked like the world was a ripe
peach and he was ready to bite it. For some reason, it
startled her. It reminded her of something she couldn't
quite put her finger on.

She suddenly thought of a conversation she'd had with one of her father's fellow teachers, Mrs. Peirce, at his funeral. She'd told Willa that Ham had been something of a ladies' man before he'd married Willa's mother, which at the time Willa had found hard to believe. But Mrs. Peirce had insisted that when Ham had come back from college, there had been something about him. She'd said Ham's mother had been very strict with him as a boy, and he'd been quite shy. But he'd been transformed by adulthood. Female teachers had clustered around him in the faculty lounge and would bring him sweets they'd stayed up all night making—divinity and angel food cake, wedding balls and honeymoon pie. Occasionally, he would invite one of them on a date, and it would leave the recipient of his attention unable to leave footprints for days, as if her feet weren't quite touching the ground. Mrs. Peirce had also said that Ham's female students were all so in love with him that sometimes they would cry over their Bunsen burners in his classroom and leave locks of their hair in his desk drawers. She'd even mentioned a small scandal involving some mothers of students who had lobbied for an advancement in Ham's career. Although he'd been perfectly happy as a teacher, they'd wanted him to become dean, principal, superintendent, and they hadn't been above blackmailing others. He'd been so charismatic in those days, Mrs. Peirce had said wistfully.

Now, looking at this photo, Willa could finally understand what Mrs. Peirce had been talking about. Grandmother Georgie had obviously snapped it; it was taken outside her apartment building. She, too, had seemed startled by what she was seeing. The photo was a little blurry, as though the camera had moved just seconds before she'd clicked it.

Willa looked through the rest of the photos, but she found herself coming back to this one. She was supposed to be looking for clues, anything that proved her grandmother didn't have anything to do with the skeleton on the hill. Her father's photos weren't going to help her. She should just put the album away and go on to the next box.

But she continued to come back to this one photo. Why did it seem so familiar, as though she'd seen it recently?

Finally, she took it out of the album and set it on the coffee table.

She went through the rest of the boxes in a matter of hours. As she'd suspected, there was nothing from her grandmother's time at the Madam here. She was going to have to figure out some other way to get information.

Willa got to her feet with a groan and a hop. She'd been sitting on the floor so long her leg had fallen asleep. She went to the front door to make sure it was locked, then turned off the living room lights. She limped to the kitchen to get something to drink before going to bed. When she opened the refrigerator, light sliced through the dark kitchen, telescoping all the way to the kitchen table at the far end of the room. She stood in front of the open door and drank some juice out of the bottle. When she finished, she put the bottle back and turned.

That's when she noticed it.

Leaving the refrigerator door open for light, she walked to the kitchen table. She had a few soft, over-ripe peaches in a hand-thrown bowl one of her National Street friends had made for her. The fruit was starting to fill the air with the sweet premonition of decay.

Her scalp suddenly tightened, and she backed away.

Propped against the bowl was the photo of her father, the strangely roguish photo she'd taken out of the album and placed on the coffee table in the living room.

And she hadn't moved it here.

Willa never thought she'd ever find herself doing this, never once thought she'd put any stock in those superstitions her grandmother had taken so seriously, but she'd been scared enough after finding her father's photo in the kitchen last night to put a penny on her windowsill and crack the window, because her grandmother had once said that ghosts often forgot they were ghosts and would go after money, but if they got close enough to an open window, the night air would suck them out.

Needless to say, she didn't get a lot of sleep. It didn't help her nerves when, that morning, a black-and-yellow bird managed to get in through the crack in her bedroom window, and it took an hour and a broom to get it to fly back out.

It was Rachel's day off, so when Willa got to the

store, she unlocked the door and turned on the lights; then she ground beans and started the coffeemaker. She wasn't as good a barista as Rachel was, but she got by. Rachel had left the case stocked with mocha-chip cookies and cappuccino doughnuts. She'd also left Willa a special box of coffee-coconut bars, which she knew were her favorite. On the box was a note: *Made these especially for you. Call me if you need me.* She must have stayed late last night just to do this.

Willa had walked in feeling moody and distracted, but this made her smile. Rachel's coffee magic was a cure for all ills, if a little hard on the waistline. It helped Willa focus, to see reason—of course, she must have moved that photo herself; she just didn't remember—and she decided on another plan of action.

The first lull in customers she had, Willa called her friend Fran at the library. Fran was a transplant and a frequent visitor to Willa's shop. She went hiking in Cataract nearly every weekend.

"Hi, Fran, it's Willa."

"Willa! This is a surprise." Fran was one of those people who always sounded like she was talking with her mouth full. "What can I do for you?"

"How do I find out what went on in this town during 1936? What kind of archives do you have?"

"Police and reporters came in here asking the same thing when the skeleton turned up at the Madam," Fran said. "Unfortunately, there wasn't a town newspaper back then. Why do you want to know?"

"I've been going through my grandmother's things, and there's not as much there about her life as I had hoped. Nineteen thirty-six was a big year for her. Her family lost the Madam. She gave birth to my father."

Fran seemed to think about it for a moment. Willa heard the tick of what sounded like computer keys. "Well, we do have several decades' worth of *The Walls of Water Society Newsletter*. That's what I showed the police."

"What is that?"

"A weekly single-page gossip column, basically. It circulated for most of the 1930s and '40s." Fran laughed. "You should read these things. They're priceless. They document the lives of the society ladies during that time."

"Do you think I could take a look?" Willa asked.

"Of course. I'll be happy to set you up."

A couple of tourists walked in, and Willa smiled and waved at them. "How late are you open today?" she asked Fran.

"It's a half-day today. Budget cuts have meant shorter hours. I'm actually about to lock up and go home." Fran paused. "I'll tell you what, call me at home when you get off work, and I'll meet you here."

"You're the best, Fran. Thanks."

ॐ

Fran was waiting for her that evening when Willa got to the library, which had recently been moved to a strip mall from its former location in the basement of the courthouse. She was standing by the door, faintly disheveled and smelling oddly of celery.

Once inside, Fran gave Willa all the microfiche film

she needed, then told her to make sure the door was locked when she left. When the heavy door shut behind Fran, Willa stood there for a moment. It was a curious sensation, being in a library alone. It made her feel like she had cotton in her ears. She walked to the microfiche readers in the back of the room, afraid to make too much noise. She sat down, and gradually the click and burr of the machine became a calming rhythm as she went though the film.

It took a while to find the 1936 issues, but when she found them she started in January and worked her way through.

The Walls of Water Society Newsletter was obviously the labor of love of a rich, childless woman named Jojo McPeat. The single-page newsletter was full of gossip from social events, usually with one or two photos included.

The events read like this:

> Mrs. Reginald Carter and her daughter made a splash in their matching pink coats at the Ingram family's annual January snow ball. Overheard by the ice sculptures were several ladies who thought the pair looked like cotton candy, but most enjoyed their ensembles, complete with matching earmuffs and hand-warmers.

Jojo made long-running commentaries on what women wore, and she loved to quote anonymous naysayers. What Willa found interesting were the small references to the town itself hidden in the text. Several of the parties' hosts would hold raffles, and the proceeds would go to local logging families that had been hurt financially when the government bought the forest surrounding Walls of Water. Jojo once quoted Olin Jackson, who was Georgie's father, at a party, promising that since the Jacksons gave this town an economy once, they would do it again, although he didn't say exactly how. And Jojo herself questioned this (allegedly drunken) statement by asking how a man who let his daughter dress in last year's clothes was going to save the town. There were jabs made toward the Jacksons quite often, but they were like pebbles being thrown at kings. The Jacksons were, unquestionably, town royalty, even if it appeared they were suffering financially.

Sitting there, Willa found herself leaning in to get a closer look at the grainy black-and-white photos of her grandmother at these parties, her breath catching in her throat at the unexpected gift of getting to see her grandmother like this. She was a stunning young woman, but her smile made her seem like she either didn't know or didn't care that she was beautiful. She looked vivacious and innocent, and she was always surrounded by her girlfriends. Agatha Osgood, herself a handsome young woman in a more reserved and angular way, was regularly at her side.

Through these photos of Georgie, Willa found herself transported. She could hear the laughter, taste the perfume in the air, smell the tobacco. She was so wrapped up, she could almost tell what the girls in the photos were thinking. She could tell when one had just danced with a boy she liked and had run back to the group to tell them, when they were discussing clothes and exasperating relationships with their families. They were so carefree and happy. Their futures were sparkles in the air, waiting to be caught like fireflies.

And then Tucker Devlin arrived.

Jojo first mentioned him in February 1936 as a salesman of ladies' cosmetics, from whom Mrs. Margaret Treble had bought a tonic and swore it made her skin feel like silk. Mrs. Treble had invited Tucker Devlin to escort her to a ladies' lunch to sell his wares, and everyone seemed to fall hopelessly under his spell. Jojo quoted Tucker Devlin as saying: "I come from a long line of peach-tree farmers, born and raised in Upton, Texas, and proud of it. I love making women feel good about themselves, but this is just a job. What I know, what I'm best at, is peaches. Peach juice swims in my veins. When I bleed, it's sweet. Honeybees fly right to me."

The first photo of him was in front of a table where he had displayed his pots and potions. He was obviously giving the ladies his spiel. Willa squinted at the photo. That was definitely the same man wearing the fedora in the photo found buried at the Madam. Her skin prickled with a sense of déjà vu, but she shook it off.

From that point on, not a single newsletter passed without mention of Tucker Devlin. And there was a gradual progression in the photos. They started out with Tucker posing with older ladies, but then he was introduced into society and he started to favor the younger women. There were numerous photos of him with Georgie and Agatha. He was kinetic. A force. Peo-

ple seemed unconsciously drawn to him. Over time,
the women in the photographs began to get desperate,
hungry looks on their faces. If it was a group shot, there
was always one girl looking at another girl with narrowed, jealous eyes.

Several newsletters later, Jojo mentioned in passing
that Tucker Devlin was living at the Blue Ridge
Madam, which startled Willa.

He had *lived* there?

It took a while to piece together through the
newsletters what had happened. Apparently, Olin Jackson got wind of Tucker Devlin's former profession, or
maybe Tucker Devlin himself approached Olin Jackson. Either way, a plan was hatched to turn Jackson
Hill into a peach orchard. Jobs would be generated.
The Jacksons would save the town again. Olin had invited Tucker to live with them while they created this
new empire.

Willa couldn't help but wonder why anyone would
plan a peach orchard at this elevation. If Tucker Devlin
was who he said he was, he would have known that
peaches wouldn't grow here. He would have known it
was a venture that was bound to fail.

And yet he had convinced everyone that it was possible.

He was a con man, just like Agatha said.

But why kill him just for that? Who was he really
hurting?

Throughout the summer, Tucker, now the town's
golden boy, appeared in the newsletter, and his favorite
escorts at parties were always the same young ladies,

with one notable exception. Curiously enough, though Georgie's friends were his constant companions, Georgie herself seemed to have disappeared from society. There were mentions of her feeling under the weather, but after May of that year, there wasn't another photo of her to be found.

Then, in August, Tucker Devlin disappeared as well. There was no explanation. There was also no mention of what had happened with plans for the orchard. Later, Willa found a short note that said the Jackson family had left the premises of the Blue Ridge Madam, per a court order. The government had seized the house for failure to pay taxes. That was October 1936, two months after the body had been buried, if the Asheville newspaper buried with the body was anything to go by.

That meant Georgie and her family had indeed still been living in the Madam at the time of his death.

That wasn't what Willa had been hoping to find. And if the police had looked at these, as Fran had said, then they knew this, too.

Willa printed out all the 1936 newsletters, then gathered the papers, turned off the lights, and locked the door behind her. She felt like she was the last to leave a party that no one really wanted to leave, but she had been hanging on the longest. As she walked across the parking lot to her Jeep, she thought she saw a few silver party streamers float into the night sky.

But she blinked and they were gone.

NINE

Root Systems

It was hard to ignore the big black Mercedes parked in front of her house.

Willa pulled up behind it and got out, and found Colin sitting on the creaky swing on her porch. Moonlight was filtering through the trees, which made the air look like milk glass. Her grandmother used to say something about how the air around you will turn white when things are about to change. It gave her pause as she watched Colin glide slowly, one hand over the back of the swing. He was one of those men for whom all their fatigue went to their eyes in a sleepy, sexy kind of way. And he was exhausted, by the looks of him.

So of course he was on her front porch?

Surely he didn't want to sleep on her couch again.

What was it about her couch and Osgoods? *She* hadn't even slept on it yet.

"I like this neighborhood," Colin said, when she reached the front porch. He'd watched her, silent, as she'd walked here. Maybe he'd felt it, too—that curious charge in the air. "It's old and quiet."

"But they don't appreciate Springsteen."

"Tragic."

Willa stopped at her door, keys in hand. "What are you doing here?"

He stood. His knee popped. "The police finally cleared the scene at the Madam for the tree planting tomorrow. I wanted to make sure you were coming."

He'd asked her before, and she still didn't understand. "What's the big deal about planting this tree?"

He shook his head as he walked over to her. "I'm going to bring out your inner nature girl if it kills me."

She unlocked the door. "You certainly have strong opinions about how I should live my life."

"I can be very persuasive," he said from behind her, close enough to her ear that she realized he was only inches away.

"Well, cross nature girl off your list. It's already been tried," she said, opening the door and walking in instead of turning around and facing him in that odd white air. She flipped on the living room light.

"Tried? By whom?" he asked as he followed her in.

She set her bag and the printouts from the library on the coffee table. "My friend Rachel. She came through here while hiking the Appalachian Trail. She's tried to get me to understand it. I just don't."

"We'll see," he said, as if there was some sort of compromise to be had. He looked around at all the boxes in the room. "What's all this? Are you moving?"

"No. These are my grandmother's things I brought down from the attic." She walked toward the kitchen, saying, "I haven't eaten since lunch. I'm going to fix a sandwich. Do you want one?"

"No, thank you," he said as he joined her. "I've already eaten. Dinner together is still mandatory at Hickory Cottage. I don't know how Paxton stands it."

It was clear he thought dinner with his family should have its own level in hell, but she thought it sounded nice. "Dinner together with your family doesn't sound so bad to me."

"Maybe it isn't. Maybe it's residual resentment." His voice sounded weary. He pulled out a chair at the kitchen table and sat. He saw the photo that was propped against the peach bowl, and lifted it. She'd left it there because she was almost afraid to touch it, almost waiting to see if it would move on its own again. "This is a nice photo of your dad."

"Yes," she agreed simply, not looking at it. She opened the refrigerator door.

"He was proud of you, you know."

She recognized that for what it was, a platitude. Because how would he know what her father felt for her? "No, he wasn't. But I knew he loved me anyway."

He watched as she brought out bread, turkey, bean sprouts, and cream cheese. "I'm sorry I haven't been in touch since Friday."

Willa set the sandwich stuff on the counter, then

reached to the open shelf above her and retrieved a purple plate. "There's nothing to be sorry about."

"It was a shock, seeing that skull. Are you all right?"

"Yes. Of course." She paused as she brought out a knife and smeared some cream cheese on two slices of wheat bread. Without looking at him, she added, "Woody Olsen came to see me on Sunday about it."

"He did? Why would he do that?"

He sounded surprised. She looked over her shoulder at him. He didn't know about Woody suspecting her grandmother. That probably meant Paxton hadn't told him about Agatha claiming responsibility for the skeleton, either. She suddenly had hope that she and Paxton were on the same page about this—say nothing until they knew more. "He wanted to know if my grandmother ever talked about anyone being buried on the hill. She didn't."

"Is that why you brought down the boxes?"

"Yes," she said, then changed the subject as she went back to constructing her sandwich. "You look tired. You must have had a rough weekend."

That made him laugh. "I'm still trying to get a good night's sleep. It keeps eluding me. But my weekend wasn't nearly as rough as Paxton's. What exactly happened that night she slept over here?"

"She didn't tell you that, either?"

"Either?" he said. "What else didn't she tell me?"

"Nothing."

Colin hesitated before he asked, "I know you and Pax aren't exactly friends, but you didn't get her drunk on purpose, did you? Like a prank?"

She turned around. He thought it was *her* fault? "I didn't even . . ." She paused, not knowing how to explain herself and not give Paxton away. She finally said, "No, it wasn't a prank. And now I'm confused. I thought your belief in my latent wild nature was what you liked best about me."

"I like a lot of things about you."

She turned back around and finished making her sandwich, flustered now. "You shouldn't come to see me when you're so tired. I think you say things you probably wouldn't otherwise."

She heard the scrape of the chair legs as he got up. "Did it occur to you that that's why I come to see you when I'm tired?" he asked as he approached her.

He appeared beside her, watching her as she put the lid back on the cream cheese and brushed some stray sprouts into the sink. He reached out and pushed some hair behind her ears. The gesture was tender, but it hit her with an unexpected force, like when you're in the ocean and a wave hits you. It's so soft and cool that it surprises you that it has such strength. Water seems so harmless that way.

"Come to the tree planting tomorrow," he said.

She finally looked up at him. Bad idea. There were those tired, dark, sexy eyes, looking at her and seeing someone she didn't think she was anymore. "Why?"

He smiled. "It's all part of my seduction."

She let that penetrate, thinking of the way he'd pressed against her that day the ground shook at the Madam. "So this is a seduction now?"

Slowly, he leaned in to her, his eyes open, searching

her face. Obviously, he found what he was looking for, because he leaned in farther and touched his lips to hers. She could feel herself sigh, immediately swept up in his current. It took no effort on her part. The force of whatever it was he was feeling overtook her. He angled closer, his hands cupping her cheeks as he deepened the kiss. She loved the rush, how it filled her, how it made her heart race in a way that wasn't fear or anxiety—which was how she used to achieve this feeling—but simple, raw pleasure.

She was now leaning back against the counter, her hands in his hair, trying to bring him closer, wanting more of this. She shifted slightly, and the knife she'd just used suddenly clanged to the floor.

They broke apart at the sound.

For a moment, they just looked each other in the eye. Colin's hands were still on her face. His thumbs brushed along her cheekbones once before he stepped back. "Yes, this is a seduction now."

"Maybe I don't want to be seduced." After what had just happened, they both knew she was lying, but he had the good grace not to call her on it.

"Then what do you want, Willa?" When she didn't answer, he smiled and said, "I'll look for you tomorrow."

Then he left.

Just days ago she'd had the answer down pat. She would have said that what she wanted was to put the past behind her and live a nice, quiet life.

Now she wasn't so sure.

How exactly do you seduce a person with a tree planting? That, ultimately, was what made her go. Willa left
Rachel to man the store, then she drove to Jackson
Hill, only to have to park at the base of it and walk up,
because the road had been blocked off to traffic. That
was surprising.

Even more surprising were all the people there. Lining the hill all the way to the Madam were onlookers,
photographers, and even a television crew, waiting for
the tree to arrive.

How many people was he planning to seduce today?
This was obviously a bigger deal than she'd thought.

When she reached the top of the hill, she stopped
and looked up at the house. She tried to imagine her
grandmother at seventeen, living here in genteel
poverty, when this charming con man moved in and
promised to save them all. Had Georgie fallen in love
with him? *Had* he gotten her pregnant? No, of course
not. Her mind simply wouldn't go there. But what if
Agatha had fallen in love with him? What if she and
Georgie had become rivals? Maybe that's why she
killed him.

The mound of dirt where the peach tree had been
was still clearly visible. It suddenly occurred to her that
her grandmother had to have known what happened.
Hadn't the newsletters said she'd disappeared from society that summer? That meant she'd been here,
watching everything. *She knew what Agatha did.* And
she'd never said a thing.

Still surveying the house, her eyes landed on Paxton, who was talking to a counselor from one of the

surrounding summer camps subsidized by the Osgood charity trust. The camp kids were all waiting with banners they'd made, welcoming the tree.

Paxton saw her there but turned away. Willa couldn't look at Paxton now and not see a little bit of Agatha, not wonder what had happened between their grandmothers that summer.

The beeping of some machinery drew her attention to the gigantic hole in the side yard of the Madam, and the scores of men and equipment surrounding it. She finally found Colin, pacing around the yard on his cellphone. At one point he said something into the phone, hung up, then went to the precipice of the hill.

Willa followed his stare and realized he was looking out over the highway. The call was probably an ETA on the tree. Sure enough, the tractor-trailer soon appeared, slowly coming down the highway, which had been closed to traffic just to transport it here. There were actually police cars as escorts, their blue lights on. It was an unexpectedly resplendent sight, something that made her chest feel full. There was a majesty to this old tree, standing proudly on the back of a modified flatbed.

It took almost forty-five minutes from the time she'd spotted it on the highway until the truck appeared at the base of Jackson Hill and heaved its way up, groaning with the monumental weight of its load. It was even more regal up close, this oak that had lived for more than a century. Nearly forty feet tall, with a branch span that had to be at least eighty feet, it evoked cheers and applause from the people lining the hill as it passed, people who seemed to be as affected by this as she was, this crazy, noble effort to save a tree that had probably been planted during the Civil War.

The process from the time it reached the Madam and backed up to the hole was excruciatingly time-consuming. Most people left over the course of the next few hours. Willa was one of the few to stay. She couldn't leave. She was riveted.

Watching the actual planting was breathtaking, like watching a primitive battle between man and beast. The tree seemed like some great animal, fighting against the hunters trying to capture it. As the machinery lowered the gigantic root ball covered in burlap and wire, the men grabbed the ropes tethered to the limbs. They yelled, and the tree groaned and actually seemed to writhe against its restraints. The men holding on to the ropes moved in sync, running one way, then the next. They knew this animal; they knew its habits. They knew how to tame it.

And then, finally, it was in.

It was one of the most glorious things she'd ever seen.

She was certain Colin had no idea she was there. He'd never once looked up from the site. When it was over, his color was high, his clothes were wet with sweat, and he was out of breath. He looked positively orgasmic.

That's when he finally looked up and around, as if searching for someone. He found Willa in the small crowd that was left. He slowly smiled, and *bam*, there it was, that lust she'd felt last night. It was heavy and elemental. It was connected to everything around them for one electric moment. It actually made her take a step back.

How did he know the effect this would have on her, when she didn't even know herself?

It was too much, this feeling that she didn't know her own nature, her own root system, anymore.

She turned around and left.

❧

For the rest of the day, Willa felt jumpy, on edge. When she got back to work, she would give a start every time the bell over the door rang. When she got home, she kept expecting a knock on the door. She got in the shower because her skin felt hot, like a sunburn, as though she'd been exposed to something that day that had a lingering effect on her. She couldn't get rid of it.

The phone rang just as she got out of the shower. She ran to her bedroom to answer it. "Hello?"

"I think that went well today," Colin said in a low voice.

This was what she'd been expecting all day. "Yes," she said, swallowing, her mouth suddenly dry. "I think you accomplished what you set out to do."

"Take Saturday off and spend it with me."

Maybe the beauty of his being here for only a month was that she could get this itch he'd caused out of her system quickly. Then he'd leave, and she could go back to normal. That was her justification for finally giving in and saying yes.

❧

At dinner that night, Paxton's father clicked around on his smart phone, which had replaced the newspaper he used to bring to the table, and her mother chatted happily about what good news coverage the tree planting had, and how it would make up for all the negative publicity the skeleton had caused.

"I'm just glad that nasty bit of business is over," Sophia said. "It didn't reflect well on any of us. Paxton, you should hold a special meeting to tell the club that everything is fine with the Madam now. I heard a rumor that some members actually wanted to change the venue for the gala. Imagine! After the invitations have already gone out."

"Yes," Paxton said. "I heard that, too." She knew she shouldn't have said it the moment it came out.

"And you didn't tell me? I had to hear about it from Shane Easton!" Twenty-five years ago, Sophia had been president of the club, and she'd groomed Paxton to be the same. When the time came for Sophia to leave the club, Paxton had had a difficult time trying to keep her mother from still trying to control things through her. She'd been so happy the day Sophia stopped asking for every single detail of meetings the moment Paxton got home. That's not to say she didn't still expect to be kept in the loop.

Colin cleared his throat. "I'd like to make an announcement," he said. "I don't want anyone at this table setting me up with a date for the gala. I know you may be tempted to. But don't."

"But Colin, I was thinking about that nice Penelope Mayfield," Sophia said, immediately distracted.

"Ha!" Colin said, pointing a finger at their mother with the hand holding his wineglass. "I knew you were planning something. No. I refuse."

"Oh, Colin," Sophia said indulgently. Colin looked at Paxton and winked. He'd done this for her.

After dinner, Colin retreated quickly to the patio, something he had taken to doing all week. Tonight, Paxton followed him.

"I don't get it," she said as she took a seat in the lounge chair next to him.

"Get what?" Colin asked, his head back against the cushions, his eyes closed.

She tried to mimic his position but couldn't get comfortable. "Mama adores you. Daddy isn't trying to make you play golf anymore. And still you can't wait to get away."

"You should know this better than anyone, Pax. It takes a lot of energy to keep up that deflector shield."

"If you moved back, you wouldn't have to eat dinner with them every night. I do because I live with them. You'd have your own place."

"I know."

"When are you moving back?" she asked. "You don't have to live in New York for work. This could be your home base."

"I don't know if I'm ready for that yet."

"Ready for what? To be here for your family? Gee, Colin, it must be nice to be you." She had no idea why she was picking a fight with him. He didn't deserve it. He wasn't even the real reason she was upset.

"I'm here now, aren't I? You asked me, I'm here."

"For a month."

His chest rose as he took a deep breath of calming air. "I'm tired, Pax. I don't want to fight with you."

Her brother never slept well. That, at least, was something they had in common. "I don't, either. I'm sorry."

The crickets made up for their lack of conversation for a while. Clouds were rolling in, dimming the light as they passed over the moon, making it seem like a power surge. Paxton could feel her emotions mirrored in the sky. Bright surges of happiness. Dark periods of moodiness.

Paxton finally said, "It's Willa Jackson you're taking to the gala, isn't it?"

"I'm working on it," he said with a smile. He turned his head on the cushion to look at her. "What about you? Who are you going with?"

Before last week, before the kiss, she would have said Sebastian. But now she wasn't so sure. He'd volunteered at the free clinic over the weekend, but now it was Tuesday, and she still hadn't heard from him, even after leaving him an apologetic message today. She didn't like being apart from him. It left a hole in her life she didn't know how to fill, because he'd been her best friend, her only friend. But how could she look him in the eye after what happened, after knowing, definitively, that he could never give her what she'd wanted so much, what she'd wanted all her life? For a moment, she envied her brother's nice, untangled life. For a moment, she understood why he stayed away.

"I think I might go alone," she said. "There will be

too much to do for me to pay attention to a date, anyway."

"I'll be your date," he offered.

"No, get Willa to come. She should be there for her grandmother." Paxton paused. "Willa was at the tree planting today. Did you see her?"

"Yes, I saw her," he said. "I invited her to come."

Paxton gnawed at her bottom lip. "So you two . . . talk?"

"Yes. Why?"

"I guess she told you all about what happened Friday night."

"No, actually," he said. "I asked. She wouldn't tell me."

That surprised her. "She didn't tell you anything?"

He lifted his head. "I'm getting the same impression from you that I got from her. Is there more than one secret? What's going on?"

"Nothing."

Colin sighed and turned his face back up to the spotty moonlight. "That's what she said."

Late that night, Sebastian sat in the back booth of the quiet, sagging Happy Daze Diner on the highway and nursed a cup of coffee, just like he used to do when he was a teenager. The only difference now was that he didn't have a satchel of books to read well into the night.

Well, that and he was better dressed and wasn't wearing eyeliner.

His father had been an alcoholic, so Sebastian spent every hour he could away from him. He would sit at this diner on the highway, the one his great-aunt used to take him to when he was a boy, the only place she could afford, and nurse a cup of coffee and read library books until he was too tired to stay awake, then he would go home and sleep on a couch on the porch, just so he wouldn't have to face his father and his verbal abuse. He called Sebastian a fag a lot, particularly when he was drinking. Then Sebastian would get up and go to school, and hear much of the same.

"Hey, baby," Lois said, coming to a stop at his booth in the back. "I thought you might like some pie."

Sebastian smiled at her. Lois had been a waitress here since he was little. She was a wiry old woman, with painted-on lips and a crooked blond wig. She and another older lady were the only two waitresses in the place, and they wore blue polyester dresses and frilly white aprons. The place had few customers, and most were over the age of seventy. They didn't pay any attention to him. No one bothered him here, which was why this had been such a safe haven. He'd thought he'd outgrown this, but it turned out he'd been wrong.

"I'm not hungry, Lois. But thank you."

"Eat it," she said, sliding the plate on the table. "You're still too skinny. Can't hide it with those fancy suits, either."

She walked away, her orthopedic shoes squeaking on the cracked linoleum floors. Pie, to Lois, was love. And Sebastian appreciated it. The moment he'd walked back in a few months ago, he and Lois had found their old routine. She still tried to feed him. He still refused. She still let him stay as late as he wanted to. Only these days he could afford to tip her a lot more.

He pushed the pie plate to the side, then looked at his cellphone sitting next to his coffee cup.

He picked it up and listened to Paxton's message again.

"Hi, Sebastian. It's me. I haven't seen you in a few days." She paused. She was on her cellphone, probably in her car. He could hear the subtle whoosh of traffic. Engine noises. She drove like she did everything else, with confidence and purpose, multitasking along the way. "I just wanted to say I'm sorry. For everything. For Friday night. For not calling you when I got drunk and needed help. You're off the hook if you don't want to go to the luncheon and recital on Saturday. I know you don't like classical music and were only going for me, anyway. Just . . . call me and let me know you're okay. Bye."

He set the phone back down next to his coffee.

Paxton Osgood was the last thing he'd expected to happen to him when he came back to Walls of Water. It had taken a lot of courage to come back here, but he'd been convinced that finding out about Dr. Kostovo's retirement had been a sign. From the get-go he had blatantly insinuated himself in circles that had previously rejected him. Those who remembered him perhaps still looked at him oddly, but he'd slid into place so easily. More easily than he'd ever expected. No one said he didn't belong, which was exactly what he'd wanted. Yet it felt nothing like he'd thought it would. He'd been

prepared to face what he'd left behind armed with bit-
terness and haughtiness, only to find there weren't any
battles left to fight here. There were only his memories
of a confused and neglected little boy, who was too
skinny and too pretty for his father to love, who was
made fun of by the other kids and misunderstood by
everyone. So no, no battles. Only ghosts.

And Paxton.

He'd couched his sexuality a long time ago. It only
got in the way, the dissonance between what he was
and how he was perceived. And he didn't think the
issue would come up when he first met Paxton. They'd
hit it off right away, and Paxton quickly became his
friend, which in itself wasn't much of a surprise.
Women often wanted to be his friend, as if friendship
with him was something of a trophy. What was surprising was how earnest Paxton was about it, how terribly
grateful she was. She'd latched on to him as though
she'd been wandering the desert and he was her oasis.
And he had to admit it felt good to be her confidant.
She was the town's golden girl, she had everything, and
he was the one she chose to confide in. But the longer
they knew each other, the more comfortable she became in expressing affection, and he slowly began to
realize she was feeling more than just friendship. His
own feelings confused him, but then, they always confused him. He didn't know how to address what was
happening between them, and since she avoided the
subject, he'd assumed this was just temporary, and they
carried on like normal.

Until that night at her house.

He took a deep breath, then pinched the bridge of his nose.

She'd been on edge. Tired. She immediately regretted it.

That should have been it, right? But if she regretted it, and he wanted to move on from it, why were they dancing around each other? Why was she telling him he didn't have to go to social functions with her now? Why was he here, avoiding her?

Did she think she couldn't keep her hands off him?

Or was it the other way around?

He'd never expected to face this. He thought coming back here would put to bed a lot of old issues. And it had. But it had also opened up a whole new set of issues he'd convinced himself five years ago that he would never have to face again.

And he had no idea what to do now.

TEN

The Magic Man

Late Friday afternoon, Paxton couldn't take it anymore. She had to go see Willa. Why was she keeping
quiet? Was she planning on using all she knew against
Paxton at a later date? Between the drunken alterca-
tion at the Gas Me Up, Paxton's confession about Sebastian, and, most of all, Nana Osgood's outburst, the
potential for public embarrassment was enormous, and
that was the *last* thing she needed right now, more
scandal surrounding the Madam. How did she end up
so beholden to a woman she barely even knew?

Paxton drove into Willa's neighborhood and parked
behind her Jeep. She straightened her shoulders and
marched to the door and knocked. It was still light,
and the scent of summer dinners being prepared wafted
through the air—sliced tomatoes, freshly popped

beans, the sharp tang of charcoal. When Willa opened the door, the contrast between the two of them couldn't have been more obvious. Willa was comfortable and casual in jeans and a high-waisted shirt that looked like it was made out of large bandana squares. Paxton was in a beige sheath dress and tailored jacket that she sprayed regularly throughout the day with a wrinkle releaser.

"Paxton," Willa said, surprised. "Come in."

"I was worried you wouldn't be here," Paxton said as she stepped inside and Willa closed the door behind her.

"I'm always here on Friday night. Friday night is vacuuming night. The fun never ends at Casa Jackson."

Paxton adjusted the tote bag on her shoulder. "Then what were you doing out last Friday?"

"I was at a cookout I hadn't intended to go to."

Lucky for me. Paxton took a deep breath and got to the point. "Listen, Colin told me he asked you about what happened last Friday, and that you refused to tell him. He also doesn't seem to know about Nana Osgood's confession." She hesitated. "I thought you'd tell him. I've been waiting for you to tell everyone."

Willa's brows knitted. "Why would I do that?"

"It's been my experience that people take a little more joy than they should when things don't go my way."

"Well, when Colin didn't seem to be aware that the police had asked me about my grandmother, I figured we were on the same page. How do we know what really happened, anyway?" Willa asked.

"You're right. We don't know," Paxton said, relieved. "But for what it's worth, I think it's absurd that Georgie had anything to do with that skeleton. I've always liked your grandmother." There was a knowing silence. "That's okay, I know you can't say the same about mine."

Willa gave her an apologetic smile.

Paxton looked around awkwardly. There were boxes in the living room that hadn't been here last week. Her eyes immediately fell on a beautiful gray dress that was draped over one of the boxes. The fabric was beaded and looked like it was covered in twinkling stars. She stepped over to it and touched it with the reverence only someone who knew the true power of dresses could have.

"This is gorgeous. Is it vintage?" It had to be. It had the tight bustier, cinched waist, and wide skirt of something from the early 1950s.

Willa nodded. "It's apparently from 1954. It still has its tags. And it was in the original box with the card attached. It was a Christmas gift from your grandmother to mine. She kept it all this time but never wore it."

"They really were good friends, weren't they?" Paxton said, still staring at the dress.

"At one time, yes, I believe they were."

Paxton stepped away from the dress and gestured to the other boxes. "What is all this?"

"My grandmother's things. I've been going through them. You caught me in the middle of putting them back in the attic."

"Looking for answers?" Paxton surmised. Of course

she was. Georgie Jackson wouldn't hurt a fly. And Willa was out to prove it. But when it came to Nana Osgood, Paxton wasn't sure what she was capable of. And that scared her.

"I haven't found much, though," Willa said, shrugging.

"What have you found?"

"I'm not out to incriminate Agatha, if that's what you're thinking. I just want to know what happened. Nothing was the same for my grandmother after that year. And I'm beginning to think Tucker Devlin might have had some hand in it." She walked over to the coffee table and riffled through some papers there. "I found this at the library." She handed Paxton a printout of the old society newsletter. Willa tapped a grainy black-and-white photo of a man in a suit standing between two mooning teenagers. The style of their clothing looked to be 1930s or '40s. "That's Tucker Devlin. He's with Georgie and Agatha in that photo."

Startled, Paxton looked closer. Sure enough, there were her grandmother's sharp cheekbones, her large dark eyes. She looked so *happy*. Paxton couldn't remember ever seeing her grandmother happy. What had happened? Where did this girl go?

"There's something that's been bothering me," Willa said. "Do you think it's just a coincidence that the Women's Society Club was formed around the time he was killed?"

"Of course it's a coincidence," Paxton said immediately. "How could the two possibly be connected?"

"I don't know. All I know is that according to these

newsletters, our grandmothers were friends who seemed devoted to each other. Then Tucker Devlin arrived and suddenly they were competitors for his affection. He disappeared in August, when they became tight again and formed the club."

Paxton rubbed her forehead. Why did that have to make so much sense? "Please don't let that theory get out. I only have a tenuous hold on the club as it is."

"I thought we just went over this. I'm not going to tell anyone," Willa said. "Would you like something to drink?"

"Yes," Paxton said. "Thank you."

When Willa left the room, Paxton went to the couch and sat, trying not to let it remind her of how sick she'd been the last time she was on it. She set the newsletter printout back down with the other papers on the coffee table, then noticed a photo album with a single photo sitting on top of it. She picked it up and studied it. He looked so magnetic in this photo. He was the kind of man you were sure could destroy entire civilizations with only a smile. Why would her grandmother kill him?

Willa came back with two bottles of Snapple and handed one to Paxton. "Tucker Devlin certainly was handsome," Paxton said. "If our grandmothers fell for him, I can see why."

Willa looked confused. "That's not Tucker Devlin. That's an old photo of my father I found in the album. I've been debating whether or not to put it back."

Paxton looked at it again. "What?"

"That's a photo of my father."

"It is? It looks just like Tucker Devlin."

Willa set her bottle down and took the photo from Paxton and looked at it. Then she lifted the newsletter printout. She compared the two, a look of comprehension coming over her face as she sat down hard beside Paxton on the couch. "Oh, God, I was trying *so hard* not to believe it."

Seconds later, it hit Paxton, too. Georgie Jackson had been pregnant when her family lost the Madam—everyone knew that. But no one knew who the father was. Until now.

That was it. The thing that turned everything around. This wasn't just Paxton's history, the one she loved and protected, the one that gave her such a sense of belonging. It was Willa's, too. And somehow they were connected. Discovering that Tucker Devlin might be Willa's grandfather was too much to ignore. Willa needed to know what happened to her family, even if it changed how Paxton thought about her own.

"I think we need to talk to Nana Osgood," Paxton said.

❧

Agatha was sitting on the love seat in her room as the sun set that evening. She couldn't see it, but she could feel it, feel the way the warmth moved across her face in tiny increments. There was a slight hint of peaches in the air, but it didn't scare her. She was just glad Georgie wasn't cognizant enough to be aware of him now.

She didn't want to eat in the dining hall that night,

so she requested that her food be brought to her room. She liked eating her food alone. Her one last pleasure. She didn't care much for mingling with the people here, anyway. She was far too old to make friends now. No one understood her anymore.

She wasn't depressed. Agatha had never been depressed. She was much too self-possessed for that. That's not to say she liked her present circumstances, and, especially since hearing about the Madam and the discovery of Tucker Devlin's remains, she found herself more and more in the past lately.

"Nana Osgood?" It was Paxton's voice coming from the doorway.

"Paxton, what are you doing here? You just missed your brother, the tree boy. He came to visit me, finally. He brought me chocolates. What did you bring me?"

"Willa Jackson," Paxton said as she walked farther into the room. There was another set of footsteps, another form beside Paxton.

"Hello, Mrs. Osgood," Willa said. Willa had been a sneaky child. Not a mean one. Not a deceitful one. But sneaky nonetheless. Agatha had always seen it. Georgie had, too, but as with Ham, she'd been convinced that she could trample down any wild hair that reminded her of Tucker Devlin and make her family as quiet and normal as possible. It hadn't always been to their advantage. In fact, Agatha believed Ham could have gone on to great things if only his mother hadn't instilled in him such a sense of his own smallness. But Georgie had felt she was only balancing out the magical stormy nature she was scared Ham and Willa might have inherited from Tucker. They *had* inherited it, of course. That much had always been clear. But that didn't mean they would turn out badly. She should have told Georgie that.

"The two of you here together can only mean one thing," Agatha said. "You want to know what happened."

"Willa found something called *The Walls of Water Society Newsletter*. We've pieced some things together."

"The *Society Newsletter*. I'd forgotten about that." Agatha laughed when she thought of it, how important they all thought it was at the time. "Jojo McPeat published it. That woman was the nosiest person God ever created."

"Mrs. Osgood, was Tucker Devlin my father's father?" Willa asked.

That hit her in the place her heart used to be. "Figured that out, did you?"

"What happened?" Paxton asked, taking a seat beside Agatha. Willa lingered in the doorway. "Did you really kill him?"

"Yes. I did," Agatha said. For all the things she couldn't give Georgie, she could at least give her this.

"Why?"

"Because we're connected, as women. It's like a spiderweb. If one part of that web vibrates, if there's trouble, we all know it. But most of the time we're just too scared or selfish or insecure to help. But if we don't help each other, who will?"

"So you killed him *for* Georgie?" Paxton asked, and

her tone insinuated she had assumed it was for other reasons—other, less noble, reasons.

"We were once as close as shirt buttons, Georgie and I. I didn't think anything would change that. Until Tucker Devlin. You have to understand what it was like back then. It was during the Depression, and on top of that, the new national forest meant no more logging. Those of us who managed to keep our money were trying to help those who had lost theirs. When he arrived, it was like we came alive again. Days were brighter. Food was sweeter. He promised us each exactly the thing we wanted most. And we believed him. The whole town believed him. We were his captives. And we learned early on not to cross him. There was an old man named Earl Youngston who repeatedly tried to get us to see that Tucker was a con man. But after a confrontation with Tucker one day, Earl's beard grew forty feet overnight, trapping him in his bed. He was quiet after that, and had to shave six times a day.

"After a while, all the men wanted his opinion, and all the girls were in love with him. He made certain of it. Because he knew the best way to get what he wanted was to break down what made us strongest. And our friendships were what made us strong. He changed all that. That's why we were so jealous when Tucker moved into the Blue Ridge Madam with his big plans to save the town by turning Jackson Hill into a peach orchard. Not only was Georgie the prettiest of our group, but she now had him under her roof."

Agatha turned her head. She could hear the food

trolley coming down the hall. It was the only sense of anticipation she had left. Her stomach tightened with it.

"Nana?" Paxton said.

Where was she? "Oh. Well, Georgie tried to tell us what was happening. She said Tucker slept in the attic and paced a lot. She said he was restless, and it affected the whole house. She said mice fled, but birds were always trying to get in. She would say things like *He's got a mean temper* and *He won't leave me alone*. But we hated her for it, because we wanted him for ourselves. After a few months, Georgie started avoiding us. She didn't go to parties anymore. We thought she was saying we were no longer good enough for her. But she did it because she was scared and ashamed, and when we turned our backs on her, she had no one left."

"What was she scared and ashamed of?" Willa asked.

"There was no love story going on up there," Agatha said. "Tucker raped her. That was one of the reasons he wanted to move there in the first place. To get to her."

Silence from the girls. The food trolley was getting nearer.

"When she finally got up enough nerve to tell me she was pregnant, I was so angry with myself. She was my best friend, and she had tried so many times to tell me what was happening, but I let my jealousy get in the way. I could have stopped it. I could have stopped it all."

"So you killed him because of what he did," Paxton said.

"No. I killed him because he wouldn't stop doing it.

He was terrorizing her. I hit him over the head with a frying pan."

"The frying pan that was buried with him," Willa surmised.

"Yes."

"Did no one know?" Paxton asked. "Did you bury him under the peach tree by yourself?"

"Georgie knew. We buried him together. And there wasn't a peach tree there at the time. It came up later." There was a knock at the door. "He always did say he had peach juice in his veins."

"Here's your dinner, Mrs. Osgood," the food-service girl said.

"Go now," Agatha said. "I want to eat."

"But . . ." Paxton said.

"If you want to know more, come back. The story has been around seventy-five years. It's not going anywhere."

She heard the shuffle as the girls left. She liked that they were together. It gave her hope.

"Don't underestimate us. You did before, and look where that got you," she told Tucker.

"What did you say, Mrs. Osgood?" the food-service girl asked as she rolled the tray table in front of her.

"Nothing. Leave me to eat," Agatha told her. Then she added, "Both of you."

ELEVEN

Love Potion

European dance troupes, African a cappella groups, Chinese bell ringers—it didn't really matter. Every year, the Women's Society Club chose one obscure international group to sponsor for an American tour, and in return they received a special private backyard concert. It was always the highlight of the summer social season—except for this one. This season, the gala was all anyone was talking about, much to the consternation of Moira Kinley, whose year it was to host the concert.

It was barely a week until the gala, and Moira knew what she was up against. But she was smart. She was savvy. And most of all, she was Southern. So she scheduled the concert as a luncheon instead of a nighttime affair, completely different dressing situations, after all, and she managed to procure Claire Waverley as the caterer. *Everyone* wanted Claire Waverley, from the nearby college town of Bascom, to cater their affairs. Her food could affect you in magical ways. It was something you remembered fondly for years. Something you compared to every other meal you had. No one was going to pass this up, not even Paxton, who didn't normally eat in social situations, and who didn't even have a date for this one.

"Introduce yourself to Claire Waverley," Paxton's mother said to her as she followed Paxton to their front door.

"I will," Paxton said, checking her watch. She had hoped she'd have time to call Willa to see how she was this morning. Last night had been intense. But now she'd run out of time. They had agreed to meet up again at the nursing home on Sunday, though.

"Make a good impression," Sophia said.

"I will."

"Give her this." Sophia handed her a small box wrapped in beautiful blue paper and a plaid bow.

Paxton looked at it curiously. "What is it?"

"It's a gift for the caterer, a gold pin in the shape of a flower, because she works with edible flowers. And I wrote her a nice note, too."

It wasn't a gift, it was a bribe, but Paxton didn't point that out. "You really want her to cater your anniversary party, don't you?"

"It's only eight months away!" Sophia said worriedly.

Paxton had reached the door by this time. "Goodbye, Mama."

"Yes, goodbye," Colin said, appearing from out of nowhere and slipping out the door ahead of them.

"Colin! Where are you going?" Sophia called.

"To commune with nature," he called back.

Paxton walked out, and Sophia said, "Fix the strap on your heel; it's crooked."

Paxton caught up with Colin as he was walking to their father's black Mercedes. "That was entirely too easy for you," she said. "It took me ten minutes just to get to the door."

"The trick is to not make eye contact. They don't charge if you don't make eye contact."

She smiled in spite of herself. "You're in a good mood."

"Yes, I am." He looked at her thoughtfully. "But you're not. When was the last time you were in a good mood, Pax? I know you don't think I care. But I do. Nothing is going to get better until you get the hell out of this house. Find what makes you happy. Obviously, it isn't here."

No, it wasn't here. She just wasn't sure where it was. "Are you really going to commune with nature?"

"Actually, I have a date with Willa today. Which is why I have to go." He nodded in the direction behind her. "Don't keep your date waiting, either."

"I don't have a date. Thanks for pointing that out."

"Tell him that," he said as he kissed her on the cheek and got in the car.

Paxton turned to see that Sebastian had parked his car in front of hers in the round brick driveway. He was leaning against the car, his hands in his pockets.

He watched her approach, not smiling, not frowning. Definitely cautious, though.

"I told you you didn't have to come," she said, stopping in front of him.

"And I told you I'd do anything for you." He opened the passenger-side door for her. "Shall we?"

She couldn't deny the relief she felt. She hadn't been looking forward to showing up alone. "Thank you, Sebastian."

They didn't talk much on the drive. They didn't mention what they'd been doing this past week that prevented them from seeing each other or returning calls. He told her she looked beautiful in pink. She commented on his car's nice wax job. That was it. She wondered if anything between them would ever be the same. And the sad answer was probably not, because she still couldn't be this near to him and not feel that pull, that desire, that *something* that definitely wasn't friendship. It never had been. And now that it was out, there was no going back.

They pulled in front of Moira Kinley's Federal-style house, called Sourwood Cottage, and the valet for the event took Sebastian's car. They walked up the steps, and as they reached the door, he finally asked, "Who is the gift for? Moira?"

"No. It's a bribe from my mother to the caterer. She wants her for her anniversary party. At some point I'm going to have to slip away and give it to her, or I'll never hear the end of it."

When they walked inside, the maid directed them to the back of the house, where they found the club members and their guests mingling outside on the large lawn. Moira had created artificial shade on this hot day by stretching a canopy of light blue fabric, the color of the sky, across the area where the tables and stage were. Huge cooling fans blew, making the fabric billow. It was a beautiful effect. All this, and Claire Waverley, too. People were going to be talking about this for days. And Moira certainly deserved all the credit.

As Paxton and Sebastian walked toward the canopy, Paxton began to notice that there were quite a few women bearing gifts, including poor Lindsay Teeger, who was trying to balance a wok tied with a bow in one hand and a wineglass in the other. It appeared that Paxton's mother wasn't the only one who wanted Claire Waverley's culinary talents for her next party.

Moira was the first to greet them. She looked happy and proud of herself. She knew what a coup this was. "Welcome!" she said, bussing their cheeks.

"This is stunning, Moira," Paxton said. "Congratulations."

"That means a lot, coming from you," Moira said. "And just so you know, I'm not trying to steal your thunder with the gala. I'm sure it will be nice, too." She pointed to the gift Paxton was holding. "Let me guess, for Claire Waverley?"

Paxton shrugged. "My mother insisted."

"I'll tell you what I told everyone else. The kitchen is off-limits. No one allowed. I don't want Claire distracted. Sorry! But grab some wine and hors d'oeuvres, and enjoy!"

As soon as she flitted off, Sebastian leaned in and said, "These women should come with danger signs."

She smiled at that as they walked under the canopy and tried to find their table. They were soon stopped by a waiter in his early twenties, handsome, full-lipped, his eyes all over Sebastian in a blatantly sexual way. He offered Sebastian some wine. Sebastian thanked him and took glasses for himself and Paxton, handed a glass to Paxton, then led her away with his arm tightly around her waist, obviously uncomfortable.

For the next half-hour, they mingled, and eventually they ended up in a group that included Stacey Herbst and Honor Redford. Paxton was getting tired of holding the gift from her mother. She thought she was conspic-uous with it, since everyone else had given up hope and had either stuffed their gifts in their purses or put them on their tables, so Paxton excused herself to put her gift at her table, as well.

She wasn't gone long. As she made her way back, she had to admire Sebastian. He managed to make every-one else here look like they were dressed for manual labor. His suit was smoky gray, his shirt was starched white, and his tie was like water. Everything was com-pletely smooth and unruffled, and he moved like there was no resistance between him and what he wore.

She wasn't the only one watching. The cute young waiter came back, this time with a tray of appetizers. He offered the tray to Sebastian, who shook his head and turned away, taking a sip of his wine. The waiter seemed to offer the tray to the rest as an afterthought.

Paxton approached the group in time to hear one of the women say to Sebastian, "He's cute. I think he's interested in you."

"Darling," Sebastian said, when he realized Paxton had joined them again. "Before we were interrupted, we were talking about you and the Blue Ridge Madam. The pall of the skeleton seems to have lifted." Just as he'd said it would.

"Yes," Paxton said brightly, too brightly. "In your eye, Tucker Devlin." She lifted her glass as if in a toast, but the glass tipped slightly and sloshed onto Sebastian's jacket. It was the oddest feeling. She could have sworn someone had pushed the glass. But there was no way anyone could have done that without her seeing. "Oh, Sebastian, I'm sorry."

"That's all right. It's too hot for a jacket, anyway."

"Have you had too much to drink already?" Stacey asked her.

Paxton looked at her with exasperation. "No. That was my first glass."

The waiter was hurrying over, but Sebastian held up his hand and shook his head, stopping him with irritation. He handed Paxton his glass and took off his jacket and shook it.

"My great-aunt used to talk about him," Sebastian said, draping his jacket over his arm and taking his glass back from Paxton. "Tucker Devlin. She said he held the town hostage with magic when he came. You know that painting in my bedroom, the one that belonged to her, the one with the bird perched on the bowl of berries?" he asked Paxton. That caused some subtly exchanged glances. They all knew now that she'd been in his bedroom. Paxton wondered if he'd said it on purpose. "She told me Tucker Devlin came to visit her once, because he liked to court all the girls, to make sure that they were all under his spell. She said as he stood there talking to her, he reached into the painting and brought out a handful of berries and ate them right in front of her. His hand was bleeding, as if the bird had pecked it. I always thought that was the strangest story. My great-aunt wasn't one for flights of fancy. But I can't look at that painting now and not wonder if that's blood on its beak, or berry juice."

"Wait a minute. My grandmother used to talk about a magic man, too," Honor said. "A salesman who traveled through here once when she was a young woman. She said he stole hearts. Every time she told me the story, she used to say, *If a man has so much heat he burns your skin when he touches you, he's the devil. Run away.*"

This set off a slew of almost-forgotten stories that grandmothers had passed down to their granddaughters about the magic man, most of them warnings. Nana Osgood hadn't been exaggerating about just how forceful Tucker Devlin's personality had been. He was still talked about in awe, even if everyone had relegated him to fiction.

He was living on in stories, stories that had been unearthed because his skeleton had been unearthed. But a man like that deserved to never be thought of again. Why couldn't he have just stayed buried? No good had come of this.

A ripple of exclamations started to roll throughout the gathering, and Paxton looked up to see that a black-and-yellow bird had found its way under the canopy and was flying around, causing people to duck. It flew in circles for a few minutes, bumping against the canopy, until it finally made its way out.

And when it was gone, everyone had forgotten what they were talking about.

Finally, Moira asked that everyone take their seats. She gave a short self-congratulatory speech about the lunch, then almost forgot to introduce the group they had sponsored that year, a quartet of Ukrainian violinists. Lunch was then served, beautiful food garnished with edible roses and tasting of lavender and mint and lust. People closed their eyes with each bite, and the air turned sweet and cool. The quartet played ravishing melodies that were strange and exotic. There was a curious sense of longing in the air, and everyone felt it. People began to think of old loves and missed opportunities. Unlike most of these functions, no one wanted to leave. Lunch lingered for hours. The quartet went through their repertoire twice. When the plates were cleared for dessert, the quartet announced that they had to leave for the next stop on their tour that night. Everyone stretched at their tables, as if waking up. Moira, standing to the side, looked very pleased with herself.

Paxton turned to Sebastian, who was staring thoughtfully into his glass of wine. "If dessert is ready, I guess that means the caterer is leaving soon. I'm not going to get the opportunity to give my mother's gift to Claire Waverley, after all. No one is, apparently."

Someone across the table said something to her, and Paxton turned her head to answer. When she turned back, Sebastian was gone.

She looked around and found him on the periphery of the tables, talking to the young waiter who had been flirting with him earlier. Paxton looked away, a small ache in her chest.

Moments later, Sebastian leaned in from behind her and said into her ear, "I've found a way to get you into the kitchen. Come with me."

Without a word, Paxton grabbed her purse and the gift, and followed Sebastian. There were a lot of people standing now, stretching their legs, so they managed to get back into the house unnoticed.

The cute young waiter was waiting for them. "Follow me," he said with a wink and a smile.

Paxton looked to Sebastian. He'd done this just for her. "Go on," he said. "I'll wait for you in the living room."

The waiter, whose name was Buster, was both sweet and outrageous. He was working his way through culinary school in Bascom. He got her past the person sitting outside the kitchen door, a guard of some sort that Moira had posted there in order to keep Claire Waverley all to herself, like a witch in a children's story.

Paxton was so surprised and touched by Sebastian's act that as soon as she walked into the kitchen, her agenda changed in a flash. It was there so suddenly, she didn't have time to think it through. She was just going to do it. She put the gift on a shelf by the door and walked forward. She had one opportunity, and she was going to take it. Maybe she could still make this happen.

Two women were standing next to a stainless-steel prep table that was littered with flowers, making it look like bright confetti had been thrown onto it in an impromptu celebration. They were amazingly composed, as still as snow. Paxton felt a little leery as she approached them.

Rich women always have their ears to the ground, listening for the buzz of something new, something that will make them happier, younger, better. Once word of a dermatologist with a miracle cream gets out, that dermatologist is booked for months. Once a personal trainer at the gym is declared the best, everyone wants him. So it was with Claire Waverley, a beautiful, mysterious caterer who it was rumored could make your rivals jealous, your love life better, your senses stronger, all with the food she created. Her specialty was edible flowers, and once it got out that she had something no one else had, everyone wanted her. But she was notoriously hard to book.

"Claire Waverley?"

"Yes?" Claire said, turning around. She was in her forties, with beautifully cut hair and a quiet intensity.

"My name is Paxton Osgood."

"Hello," Claire said. She put her arm around the young woman beside her. "This is my niece, Bay."

"Nice to meet you," Paxton said.

Bay smiled. There was definitely a family resem-
blance. The dark hair, the gamine features. But Claire's
eyes were sharp and dark, and Bay's were bright blue.
Bay was probably fifteen—skinny, awkward, and completely charming. She was wearing so many braided
bracelets that they covered half her arm, her T-shirt
read: IF YOU ASK ME, I'LL TELL YOU, and she had an old
Romeo and Juliet paperback stuffed into the back
pocket of her jeans.

"I'm sorry to bother you," Paxton said.

"You're not. Our work is done. Dessert is ready." She
gestured to the large trays of custard cups, ready for the
waiters to pick up. "Cups of lemon crème layered with
hazelnut shortbread crumbles, pansies, lavender, and
lemon verbena."

"That sounds wonderful."

"Bay, take that box out to the van, please." As soon as
the girl was gone, Claire said, "You have a question."

She was used to this, Paxton realized. She was used
to lovesick people wanting something from her—a
cure, a potion, a promise. It was in her eyes. She'd seen
it all before. The longing. The desperation. She knew
what Paxton was going to ask before she said it.

Paxton looked over her shoulder to make sure no one
else was near enough to hear. "Can you really make
people feel differently with the food you cook, with the
drinks you prepare?"

"I can change moods. What I can't do is change people. There is no magic for that. Who are you looking to
change?"

The words brought her up short. She didn't want

Sebastian to change. And being in love wasn't something that was wrong. She couldn't, wouldn't, change that. She realized this was her last-ditch effort to make things go her way. Find what makes you happy, her brother had said. This didn't bring her happiness, so why was she pursuing it? It was time, she realized, to finally give up. "No one, I guess," Paxton said.

Claire gave her a small, understanding smile. "It's for the best. The harder we fight, the worse it gets. I speak from experience."

Paxton walked out of the kitchen, a little numb. But that was okay. She actually preferred it. She walked to Moira's living room to find Sebastian.

Despite his delicate features and slim build, he could give off such a lord-of-the-manor vibe when he wanted to, lofty and untouchable. That's what he looked like now, sitting on the leather couch, staring out the window. He turned when he heard her approach.

He looked surprised. "You didn't give her the gift."

Paxton looked at the wrapped box in her hands. "No. I think I'd like to go home."

He uncrossed his legs and stood. He grabbed his jacket from the back of the couch and walked toward her silently. Once outside, Sebastian gave the valet his ticket. To the right, Paxton could see the Ukrainian performers climbing into a large white van. Without another thought, she went over to them and handed them her mother's gift and said, "Thank you. It was beautiful."

They smiled, not understanding these strange Southern American women.

The valet had delivered Sebastian's Audi by the time she walked back. Sebastian helped her in, then got behind the wheel.

Before he could start the engine, she said, "I almost asked Claire Waverley for a love potion."

He sat back slowly and looked at her. "Almost?"

"I don't want you to be something you aren't. You're wonderful just as you are. And my feelings are inconvenient, but they're not wrong. I don't think I would change them, even if I could."

With a sigh, he leaned over and put his forehead to hers, then closed his eyes. He, too, seemed to understand the hopelessness of the situation. After a moment, he pulled back slightly and looked at her. His eyes traveled all over her face and then slowly, almost imperceptibly, he leaned in to her again, watching her mouth. This had to be all her doing, somehow. She was creating this because she wanted it so much. "Don't do this," she whispered, when his lips got close enough that she could smell the slight tang of wine from his last sip in his glass. "Don't pity me."

His eyes darted to hers, confused. "What makes you think I'm pitying you?"

"I know it's not something you want to talk about. I know you like to maintain this mystery when it comes to your sexuality. But I saw you, remember? Back in high school, our senior year. You were with a group of boys in the food court in the Asheville Mall. One of them leaned over and kissed you, and you looked right at me." He leaned back in his seat, startled. She missed his nearness instantly, so much that she wanted to curl into herself to keep the last bit of his warmth with her. "I will never ask you to be something you're not. Never. I know you can't feel for me what I feel for you. So it's my problem. It's my roadblock to get around. Not yours."

He took a deep breath and shook his head. "I'd forgotten about that," he said.

There was an uncomfortable pause before he started the car and pulled out. He drove to an intersection and came to a stop, and Paxton recognized the car that had stopped to their left. It was Colin, with Willa in the seat next to him. Colin honked and waved at her.

If she didn't love her brother so much, she'd probably resent him.

He'd obviously had a much better day than she had.

TWELVE

Strange Seductions

Rachel Edney believed that she was, essentially, a practical person. She did not believe in ghosts or superstitions or bells that could ring on their own.

But one thing she did believe in was love. She believed that you could smell it, that you could taste it, that it could change the entire course of your life.

And she was living proof.

She'd never lived in one place for more than a year while she was growing up. And she'd been all set to follow that same pattern into adulthood. There was nothing wrong with it, after all. Stability was overrated. Crises and adventures, on the other hand, could actually teach you something. A year and a half ago, she'd hiked through Walls of Water, broke and tired. She'd decided to stop and get a job long enough to stock up on some cash, and then leave again. She'd easily found work at the sporting goods store because, let's face it, you can't spend your childhood living in campground after campground without knowing a little about what you need to survive. Willa, the store's owner, had seemed relieved. Rachel liked Willa. She was nice and funny, but so full of unexpressed emotion that Rachel had tried everything she could to pop her balloon just to let some of that pressure out. Nothing ever worked, which was strange. Rachel wasn't usually wrong about people.

Even after finding work, Rachel had had to camp illegally in Cataract because she couldn't afford to rent a place. That's where she'd been discovered one rainy night by a park ranger named Spencer. He hadn't really wanted to make her leave, so he'd agreed to let her stay until morning if she'd promise to pack up and leave at first light. She'd been so grateful that she'd kissed him right there, standing in the rain. He'd been uptight and embarrassed about it. He'd actually blushed as he walked away. But when he came back the next morning, he'd seemed relieved to find her there, even after he'd told her to go. And that's how it happened.

Rachel fell in love, and it changed everything.

She'd lived here longer than she'd lived in any other place, which was an odd feeling for her. But Spencer was here—sweet, kind, stable Spencer—and she knew she couldn't be anywhere he wasn't, which, when she thought about it, was exactly how Rachel's mother had found herself trailing Rachel's father around the country. So she got used to this curious place and its funny superstitions. She got used to sleeping on a mattress and using a crockpot. She learned to drive. She even got Willa to let her open the coffee bar in the store. And to her surprise, she was really good at it.

Coffee, she'd discovered, was tied to all sorts of memories, different for each person. Sunday mornings, friendly get-togethers, a favorite grandfather long since gone, the AA meeting that saved their life. Coffee *meant* something to people. Most found their lives were miserable without it.

Coffee was a lot like love that way.

And because Rachel believed in love, she believed in coffee, too.

But that was all.

She still didn't believe in bells ringing on their own, even though the one in the store kept doing it.

She looked up when it rang again that Saturday, expecting to see no one there, but to her surprise, it was Willa.

"What are you doing here?" Rachel asked. "It's your day off."

"I'm going out with Colin Osgood today, and he's meeting me here," Willa said, walking up to Rachel at the coffee bar. "If you start making kissy noises, I will strip you of all your coffee privileges."

Rachel pretended to think seriously about it, then asked, "Can I make a joke?"

"No."

"A limerick?"

"No."

"Can I hum the 'Wedding March' as you leave?"

"No."

"Does this mean you and Colin are—"

Willa stopped her before she could finish. "No."

"Are you sure?" Rachel nodded toward the store window, and Willa turned to see Colin walk by. "I've never seen you hide from anyone before. He must do something crazy to you."

When Colin walked in, he looked from Rachel to Willa, probably wondering why they were staring at him. He looked down as if to make sure he'd actually put on clothes that morning. He was wearing shorts, hiking boots, and a long-sleeved tee.

Rachel saw Willa's eyes narrow. "You're dressed like . . . No." She put one hand up. "Absolutely not."

"Guess what?" Colin said, grinning. "We're going hiking."

"I don't want to go hiking." Willa said. "I'm not dressed for hiking."

"Are we, or are we not, standing in a sporting goods store?"

"That's why you wanted me to meet you here!" Willa said, outraged.

"Yes."

Willa crossed her arms over her chest. "I'm not going."

"Come on. Trust me," Colin asked.

"I'll get a pair of hiking boots in your size while you change into shorts and a T-shirt," Rachel said, figuring that, between the two of them, she and Colin might just make this happen. "I'll even let you wear my straw cowboy hat."

"She'll even let you wear her hat," Colin said, looking Willa in the eye and raising his brows, as if this was the clincher.

Rachel knew that if Willa didn't want to do something, she wouldn't, so the fact that she let herself be talked into this meant the only person she was really fighting here was herself.

In a matter of minutes, she was all suited up, looking a lot like a kid forced to wear an awful outfit Grandma made. "Let's get this over with," she said. "But I already told you, this has been tried before."

"She went hiking with me once, saw a snake about ten steps into the trail, and then ran back to the car," Rachel said.

Willa shivered. "I don't like snakes."

"Most snakes are nice," Colin said.

"Oh, great," Willa said as she walked to the door. "You like snakes."

Colin followed her out. "There's nothing to be afraid of. In fact, I could show you one you might like."

"I don't want to see your snake, thank you very much. Anyway, I said I didn't like them, not that I was afraid of them."

"Is that a challenge?" he asked.

"What is with you and challenges? *No*."

"Get a room already," Rachel said as they left.

"I heard that," Willa called as the door closed behind them.

Yes, Rachel Edney believed in love.

And she knew it when she saw it.

☙

They drove through the entrance of Cataract National Forest, along winding roads with savagely beautiful vistas. There were several lookouts along the way where people could park and simply stare out over the horizon. A few of the lookouts even provided views of some of the waterfalls the forest was known for. Most of the waterfalls, though, could be accessed only on foot.

When Colin parked in the gravel lot at one of the trail heads, Willa looked around and said, "Where are we going, exactly?"

"To Tinpenny Falls."

All things considered, that was a relief. Tinpenny Falls was a popular attraction, and the trail was probably not a treacherous one. She'd had septuagenarians come into her store and tell her they'd hiked the Tinpenny Falls trail. If they could do it, surely she could. "Did you ever hike these trails when you lived here?" she asked, still sitting in the car, stalling.

Colin unbuckled his seat belt. "No."

"So this is the first time you've been here?"

"No, this isn't the first time I've been here. Don't worry." He reached over and put his hand on her knee. His skin was warm against her air-conditioning-cooled leg, and it made her breath catch. "I know where we're going. When I come back for visits, I always hike. It helps me cope."

"Cope with what?"

"With being here."

Not giving her a chance to respond, he got out and shrugged on a backpack, clicking the front strap around his waist.

This was certainly a strange seduction, she thought as she got out of the car. In fact, she'd been so caught up in his challenges to how she lived her life that she'd never actually questioned what his real motivation might be. Until now. And it was quite a revelation, how little this really had to do with *her*.

Colin headed down the trail, and she reluctantly followed him into the leafy green beyond. He was a natural tour guide, pointing out interesting flora and the differences between new tree growth since the logging stopped and old growth that had been preserved. She didn't pretend to be fascinated. She mostly looked for snakes. She wasn't a nature girl, though for some reason he wanted her to be. He wanted her to be a lot of things. He'd told her that she had inspired him to leave, to follow his own path, and she was slowly beginning to understand that her life here, the fact that she came back and stayed, challenged how he'd chosen to live his own life. He didn't think he belonged here, so she was making him face some uncomfortable facts. People adapt. People change. You *can* grow where you're planted.

And Colin didn't like it one bit.

Not that she was particularly pleased to realize she'd grown to like this place far more than she'd ever thought she would.

So where did the seduction fit in? Was it only a means to an end, part of his trying to influence her to change to fit his expectations, so he could go back to thinking he'd made the right decisions in his life?

She didn't think so, but she couldn't be sure.

They stopped for water and the snacks Colin carried in his backpack, and she hadn't realized how winded she'd gotten. She was thankful for the opportunity to rest and watch the quiet progress of a group on horse-back across the river on the park's only horse trail. But once the break was over, Colin was off again.

They finally reached the top of Tinpenny Falls, and it was a magnificent sight. The river leading to the precipice of the falls was very calm and surprisingly shallow. But when the water met the edge of the rock, it roared over and dropped more than a hundred feet into a pool littered with large, flat rocks below.

This was the area's most famous waterfall, named after a handsome but boastful man named Jonathan Tinpenny. As the story went, almost two centuries ago, Mr. Tinpenny rode on horseback from his home in Charleston, South Carolina, through the rolling green mountains of western North Carolina, in search of the waterfalls he'd heard were in this area, where the waters were reportedly healing and there were claims of curative miracles. Mr. Tinpenny was only in his twenties at the time, but rheumatism came early to the men in his family. Though he suffered from this ailment, Mr. Tinpenny made the pilgrimage by himself out of pride for his supposed fortitude, because he was the youngest, tallest, and most hardy of his brothers. But he wasn't expecting the roads in the high, cool mountains to become so rough and rutted. He wasn't expecting a land of clouds. He led his horse through quagmires in the road that were waist-deep, and he filled several bottles with fog to take home with him, because he didn't think anyone would believe how thick it was. The journey was hard on him. When he found Tinpenny Falls, he was almost delirious with pain. He lost his footing and fell over. Miraculously, he survived, and he was found by hunters only hours later. He was taken home by train, where he slept most of the time in a luxuriously appointed private car. He claimed the waters must have, indeed, been healing, because look how hard his journey was on him to get there, and how easy it was on him to get home. At his funeral years later, his children opened those jars of fog he'd collected, and legend had it that fog as thick as smoke filled the city for days.

Tourists loved that story. And they loved to buy those commemorative Jars of Fog in town.

But as beautiful as it was, this obviously wasn't the destination Colin had in mind. He led her across a natural bridge of flat rocks to the other side of the falls. "What made you decide to become a landscape architect?" Willa asked, when he reached back and took her hand in his as they walked in single file.

He shrugged, still trudging forward. "There's a grove of hickory trees on my parents' estate, long rows of trees with their branches stretching into each other, constantly having to be cut back. I remember going out there when I was a boy and lying under them and just staring up at the canopy. My mother used to call it my thinking place. There was an uneasy symmetry to them. Their chaos was given structure by the landscapers, but that structure was always threatened by their own wild nature. I decided landscaping was like lion-taming," he said, looking over his shoulder with a smile. "But I didn't decide to go into landscape architecture until after I graduated from college. My undergraduate degree is in finance, which is what my dad wanted, because that was his degree, too. But after college, just as an excuse not to go home, I went on a tour of Europe with my girlfriend at the time, and the castle gardens there sort of reawakened my desire to lion-tame." He paused. "And then there was you."

"Yes," she said, knowing where this was going. "And then there was me."

"I was pretty miserable in college, and I remember thinking to myself, *Willa Jackson is probably doing exactly what she wants to do with her life right now.* You went out with such a bang."

"This may come as a surprise to you, Colin, but I wasn't any more happy when I left than when I was here. I was wild and irresponsible and flunked out of college. I was working as a gas station attendant and was two weeks away from losing my apartment when my dad died. I don't know what would have happened if I hadn't come back."

"You never got the chance to find out," he pointed out.

"No. Coming back and facing everything was exactly what I needed to do. And if I ever leave here again, I can do it with confidence. I won't be running from it."

That made him stop and turn to her. "Is that what you think I did?"

"I don't know," she answered honestly. "But here's some advice you don't want to hear: Spend more time here and maybe people will see you as you are now, and not as the Stick Man."

"You sound like my sister."

"Don't give Paxton a hard time," Willa surprised herself by saying. "She's got a lot on her plate."

"So now you're bosom buddies?" he said, smiling as he took her hand again. "We're almost there."

He led her off the trail and through the woods, and eventually they stopped at a small tributary of the river they'd just crossed. It trickled down a very large, flat rock and into a forest pool.

Colin took off his backpack and threw it to the bank below. Then he sat down and unlaced his boots. "You know, the reason they say Jonathan Tinpenny survived is not because he fell off the falls but that he actually slid down this rock instead."

"What are you doing?" she asked suspiciously.

"Just taking off my boots." He stood and tossed his shoes down, too.

She suddenly understood what he was going to do. "Did you see those signs? It said no sliding down the rock."

"No, I didn't see them," he said, walking carefully out onto the glistening rock. "I never see them."

"You've done this before?"

He sat down and scooted to the edge, sucking his breath at how cold the water obviously was as it flowed over his legs. "Come on, Willa. I dare you."

"You think that's all it's going to take. A dare?"

"I know you want to."

"You cannot possibly know that."

"Until you can tell me exactly what you do want, I'm going to make it up as I go along." And with that, he propelled himself forward and went sliding down the wet rock.

"Colin!" she yelled after him.

He splashed into the water, disappearing for a moment. Then he resurfaced, shaking his head and flinging water out of his hair. He looked up at her. "Come on! The water feels great."

"We're going to get arrested!"

He floated on his back, still staring up at her. "That didn't used to stop you."

Staring down at him, her fingers twitching with the thought of what a rush it would be to slide down this rock, she realized that yes, there *was* some of the Joker left in her. Probably always would be. And when she acknowledged that, she could finally see how little there was left of it. Enough to get her into trouble every once in a while, to satisfy this crazy need to feel her heart pound with adrenaline, but not enough to ruin the life she'd made for herself. And that made her feel better, not quite so afraid of herself anymore. And not so afraid of Colin, either, and all that she thought he'd known about her just because she hadn't had the courage to look there herself.

What an absolutely *freeing* epiphany.

So this was what she was going to do. She was going to take her boots off and throw them to the bank below. Then she was going to scoot onto the large, flat rock. She was going to slide on the water into the pool below, and enjoy it every moment. She was definitely going to come up laughing.

And that's exactly what she did.

After a lot of swimming and flirtatious playing, they finally lifted themselves onto a rock on the bank to dry themselves in the sun. They stretched out side by side in comfortable silence. Willa was almost certain that Colin felt smug about getting her to do this. But she was feeling too good to call him on it. The rock was warm underneath her, the gentle sound of the water was lulling, and the forest smelled of mulch and green leaves, of both the past and the future. She wasn't much of a nature girl, but she could get used to this.

"There's something I've been meaning to ask you," Colin said.

Willa turned her head on the rock. He'd taken off his T-shirt, and his bare chest was tan and taut. His eyes were closed, so she felt free to study him at her leisure. She'd never spent time with someone so tall. There was so much of him. "Yes?"

"What makes you think your father got fired?"

That surprised her. "Because he never went back to teaching."

"I was there the day he left," Colin said. "And he wasn't fired. He quit."

Willa sat up and turned to him. "What?"

Colin opened his eyes, then lifted one arm to block out the sun. "When you pulled the fire alarm and then

let that banner fall, announcing that you were really
the Joker, my parents showed up almost immediately,
demanding an apology from the principal because I'd
been his number-one suspect since you put that
Ogden Nash quote on the marquee. Your father was
called in to apologize, as well. I could tell he was
upset with your being escorted out of the school by
the police. It was clear he didn't want to be there,
apologizing to us like he'd done something wrong. By
that time everyone had figured out that the reason
you'd been so successful as the Joker was because you
had your dad's keys and passwords. The principal said
to your father, 'I know it's not your fault you have a
sneaky daughter. You won't be penalized for that.' And
your father just lost it. He said that if I had pulled
something like what you had just pulled and was
caught in the act, I wouldn't have been hauled off by
the police. In fact, when everyone thought it was me,
no one took action, because of who my family was. He
said he was proud of your acts of rebellion, that he
wished he'd had the courage to do it himself when
he was your age, and that he'd known what you were
doing all along. Almost from the very beginning. He
said something about being tired of living such a cautious life and for once he was throwing caution to the
wind. And he quit."

Willa was flabbergasted. "That doesn't sound anything like my father."

"I know," Colin agreed. "But that's what happened."

"He knew?"

"Apparently so. I thought you should know."

"That makes absolutely no sense."

Colin shrugged and closed his eyes again, and it didn't take long to tell that he'd gone to sleep. She sat there, her arms wrapped around her knees, thinking about the possibility of her father actually knowing about her pranks all along, about him saying he was finally throwing caution to the wind. What did that mean? She'd always assumed he was happy with his life, happy doing what Grandmother Georgie told him to do. And she'd thought he was ashamed of her actions as a teenager.

She and Paxton had planned to meet at the nursing home tomorrow to talk to Agatha again. Maybe Willa could ask Agatha about her father and Grandmother Georgie's relationship. If it was like everything else she'd learned lately, there was a lot more going on there than she'd thought.

She didn't know how long she'd sat there, lost in thought, before she turned to see if Colin was still asleep.

He wasn't. He was staring at her, one arm propped under his head.

"Did you have a nice nap?"

"Sorry," he said as he sat up, his ab muscles tightening. "I didn't mean to conk out on you. I don't sleep well, especially when I come home. It catches up with me."

She gave him a sympathetic smile and brushed some of his dark hair off his forehead. "Yes, I noticed that when you passed out on my couch."

"That is a *great* couch."

Their eyes met, both smiling. As if by mutual

consent, Colin leaned forward and she met him halfway, their lips touching gently, sun-warm and dry. It wasn't long before gentle turned hungry and insistent. She found herself leaning back, and he went with her. She'd never felt like this with a man before. He made her chest feel like it was going to explode. God, to feel this way without actually breaking the law was amazing. Okay, so technically they had broken the law by sliding down the rock, but kissing here on the bank, this was simply living in the moment, and there was no law against that.

She felt his hand push at her shirt, and she arched against him. "You're so beautiful," he said as her shirt passed over her head, landing somewhere behind them. His hands went to her breasts, and she sucked in her breath. "I think I've always been looking for you. I can't believe you've been here all along."

He pushed her bra to the side and kissed her breasts. She opened her eyes and focused on the top of the rock. Someone could come along at any moment. "Colin, someone might see."

He lifted his head. "And tell me that doesn't excite you on some level," he said as he put his lips to hers.

She pulled at his hair until he lifted his head again and looked down at her. He was breathing heavily. "It excites me now, who I am now, Colin," she said, because, for some reason, it was important for her to tell him. "This isn't me being someone I used to be."

He looked confused.

She suddenly felt sad. This wasn't going to be what she wanted it to be. How could it? It was built on too many misconceptions. "You're not going to stay, are you?" she asked.

He hesitated a moment before he said, "No."

"So your plan is to seduce me and then leave."

"There was no plan." His eyes bore into hers. "Why don't you come with me?" He wasn't a disingenuous man. In her heart, she knew that. He was trying to find a way to make this work.

"I can't leave now. My grandmother is here."

"Look me in the eye and tell me you're happy, Willa."

Disingenuous, no. Astoundingly unaware, yes. "Why don't you do the same?"

He lifted himself off of her so quickly it was almost as if she'd slapped him. "Of course I'm happy."

She readjusted her bra and found her shirt and put it on. "Right. That's why you sleep so well."

He used both hands to scrub his face, as if finally waking up. He sighed and watched the water for a moment. "We should go," he said, reaching over and handing her her boots.

Well, at least one of them had learned something about themselves on this hike.

Too bad it wasn't him.

They followed Tinpenny Trail back around to the trailhead. It was mid-afternoon, and the sun was slanting through the trees by the time they reached the parking lot. They climbed inside his car, and Willa left her window down to let the warm summer wind blow on her as Colin drove.

"Are you hungry?" he asked, the first time he'd spoken to her since the rock.

"Starving," she admitted.

"Let's get something to eat. Let's not end the day on such an uncomfortable note," he said, and she appreciated the effort.

"Have you ever been to the Depot Restaurant on National Street?" she asked. "Hikers come in looking like us all the time."

Once out of Cataract, the first intersection they came to was a four-way stop. To their right was a blue Audi.

"That's Sebastian's car," Colin said, giving them a honk and a wave. "He and Paxton must be heading home from the concert luncheon. I can't believe it went on this long."

"Do you want to ask them to join us?" Willa asked, trying not to sound too eager to have someone join them and dispel this awkwardness.

"That's a good idea," he said quickly. She guessed she wasn't the only one.

Colin got out and jogged over to Sebastian's car at the intersection. He said something to them. When he jogged back and got back in, he said, "Good call. They look like they could use a drink."

From what Willa knew of Paxton and Sebastian's relationship, she wasn't surprised. "I think we all could."

THIRTEEN

The Joker, the Stick Man, the Princess, and the Freak

They drove to National Street and parked at the old train depot, which had been the lifeblood of Walls of Water more than a century ago, when this had been a busy logging town. But when the government bought the surrounding mountain forest and turned it into a national park, the train stopped coming, and everything had to change. The depot turned into a restaurant and visitor center. The stores turned into tourist shops. And dozens of outdoor sculptures and markers were placed up and down National Street, all depicting waterfalls from the surrounding park. You couldn't walk more than ten steps on this street before encountering another reminder that this was the way to the water-falls. That this was the yellow brick road.

The Depot Restaurant was located in what was once the roundhouse in the old depot. It was full of hikers that day, their backpacks propped against their chairs. Willa, Colin, Paxton, and Sebastian walked in, an interesting foursome, to be sure—Willa and Colin with their wrinkled clothing and tousled hair, and Paxton and Sebastian a beautiful complement to each other in their dress clothes.

They were told there was a wait to be seated, but they could eat at the bar if they wanted to. They decided that was a great idea, especially since Paxton and Sebastian had already eaten and wanted only drinks.

Paxton and her brother sat beside each other, Willa and Sebastian on either side of them. Willa enjoyed watching the siblings interact. She knew they were twins, but they were so unalike that she didn't really get their similarities until she saw them together—their dark eyes, their kind smiles, the way they teased each other and sat with perfect posture.

After they had placed their orders, Colin, Sebastian, and Paxton all commented on how nice the place was. They'd never been there before.

That made Willa laugh. "You're such *townies*."

"And you're not?" Paxton asked with a smile.

"I've stretched my boundaries."

When their drink orders came, Colin turned to Sebastian and asked, "How long have you been back in Walls of Water?"

"Just a year," Sebastian said. "What about you? Any plans to move back?"

Colin carefully avoided looking at Willa and Paxton as he said, "No."

"I don't get it," Paxton said, lifting her margarita and taking a sip. "What's so wrong about Walls of Water? It's our home. We were born and raised here. Our history is here. Why would you want to be anywhere else? This place defines us."

"You hit the nail on the head right there, Pax," Colin said. Paxton and Willa both turned to him with similar expressions of exasperation.

"You don't like that this place defines you?" Paxton asked.

Colin shrugged. "I'm not the Stick Man anymore."

"And yet you still want to believe I'm the Joker," Willa said.

"The Joker was stepping out of your shell. You proved to a lot of people that there was more to you than they thought. It was a good thing." He toasted her with his glass.

"It wasn't all about proving I was more than what people thought of me. Being the Joker was a manifestation of a lot of unresolved family problems."

Sebastian snorted, and everyone turned to him. He was leaning casually against the bar. "You two had it easy. Try being the Freak sometime."

"I guess you're the only one who hasn't changed, Pax," Colin said. "And I think it's because you had yourself figured out long before any of us."

That seemed to hurt Paxton, and Willa wanted to punch Colin on the arm.

"I guess I'm just the Princess of the group, aren't I?"

"I meant that as a compliment."

"No, you didn't," Paxton said. "You want to know the real difference between me and all of you? I don't love any of you any less for not being exactly who I want you to be."

"No, you reserve that criticism for only yourself," Sebastian said softly.

Silence.

"Is it just me, or did this conversation suddenly get a little too serious?" Willa said.

They tried to laugh it off, and soon Willa's and Colin's sandwiches arrived. As they ate, Paxton told them about the magical food at the luncheon, and Sebastian told some funny stories about the society ladies. Colin, who was obviously a voracious eater with an enviable metabolism, finished his Reuben quickly.

Paxton had been turning her glass in circles on the bar, but when she noticed his empty plate, she said, "Can I ride back with you to Hickory Cottage?"

Colin wiped his mouth with his napkin. "I need to take Willa back to her Jeep first."

"It's just up the street at my store," Willa said, setting her sandwich down. "I can walk."

"Paxton, I can take you home," Sebastian said. "Willa's not finished."

"No. I think I'm finished," Willa said, and she wasn't sure why. Everyone suddenly seemed so anxious to leave that she found herself caught up in it. It was like seeing a crowd run quickly away from something. You don't stick around to see what it is. You run, too.

Paxton stood, and Colin followed suit.

"I'll see you tomorrow?" Sebastian asked Paxton.

"No. I meant to tell you. You get a Sunday reprieve. Willa and I are going to talk to Nana Osgood tomorrow."

"You are?" Colin said. "Why?"

Paxton sighed. "Maybe one day, Colin, when you're finally interested in this family, I'll tell you," she said as she walked away.

"Well, this is going to be a fun car ride home," Colin said as he left some money on the bar, covering the check.

"Thanks for the hike," Willa said.

"I'm sorry I made you go."

"I'm not." He met her eyes for a moment longer than necessary, then left.

Sebastian moved down to sit beside her. "If that's what we were saying, can you imagine what we weren't saying?" He nodded to her sandwich. "Finish. I'll drive you to your Jeep."

"That's okay. I'll walk."

"Then I'll walk you," he said.

Willa stared at her sandwich. She wasn't hungry anymore. "Let's go, then," she said as she slid off the stool. "I'm done."

It was early evening when they walked outside, the sky the color of pink lemonade. Her grandmother used to tell her that a pink sky meant someone in the distance had just fallen in love—a rare moment of whimsy from a woman who had been scared of everything. National Street was still busy, and many stores were still open as they walked down the sidewalk together. Sebastian had a calm way about him. He was someone who didn't mind silence.

"How long have you and Paxton been . . . close?" Willa finally asked him.

"Since I came back to town. We instantly connected." Sebastian didn't seem like the type who would deliberately hurt someone else. Did he know Paxton was in love with him? And was that something Willa should tell him? She had no idea why she was even considering getting involved. She guessed she didn't like the thought of Paxton being hurt by someone who hadn't entirely figured himself out yet. A little like Colin, she supposed. Not that she was hurt. Not really. Her feelings for him were her own fault. She'd always known he was leaving.

"You and Paxton seem to be getting to know each other pretty well," Sebastian commented, after another stretch of silence.

"I don't know about that. *Understand* is probably a better word. We're getting to understand each other. Our grandmothers had a connection a long time ago. We're sorting through the details."

"For the gala?" he asked.

"Not entirely."

They finally reached Willa's store. The lights were off inside, and Rachel had already left. "Thanks for the walk. This is my Jeep," she said, unzipping her cargo shorts' pocket and taking out her keys.

"You know, Colin was right about one thing," Sebastian said. "By being the Joker, you did prove to a lot of people that there was more to you than they thought. And you can't say that you didn't intend for it to happen, either, because you made absolutely certain we all knew it was you in the end, with that banner."

Willa smiled sheepishly. "Well, I thought I was never coming back to Walls of Water after college. I wanted the legend to have a name."

"You inspired me a little."

"I did?"

"Back then, I needed to break free of some things, too. I needed to stop being what everyone thought I was. But there will always be a little bit of the Freak in me. It's part of who I am."

She'd always thought of Sebastian as the master of reinvention. But she now realized that he hadn't reinvented himself at all. He'd *become* himself. "How did you come to terms with it?"

"We are who we are. It's surprising how little say we have in it. Once you accept that, the rest is easy." He leaned in and kissed her cheek. "Good night, lovely."

"Good night," she said as she watched him walk away.

Willa had already showered and had on her cotton shorts and tank top for bed when there was a knock at the door. She pulled on a short robe and walked downstairs, turning on lights she'd already turned off for the night.

When she opened the door, her favorite insomniac was there, looking absolutely miserable.

"I'm sorry," Colin said. "I'm sorry I implied that your life is anything less than what it needs to be, for you, for your family. I made this all about me."

"Yeah, I finally figured that out." She stepped back and let him enter. He brought in with him that lemon-pie scent she'd smelled once before. Regret.

"I don't know why this place affects me like it does, like I can't be myself here, even though I always am. I make a point of it. Maybe I'm just protesting too much. Maybe I think if I do come back, I won't be as good an Osgood as the rest of my family. That's always been a big fear of mine. But, God, it makes me tense just to think about it. I don't want that. I don't want society parties and days spent on the golf course." He ran both hands through his hair. It was still damp, as if he, too, had recently showered.

Willa folded her arms over her chest. "Has anyone actually made you do anything you didn't want to do since you've been coming back for visits?"

He frowned. "Well, no."

"So you're just rigidly creating conflict that isn't there." She laughed. "Guess what, Colin? There's still some of the Stick Man in you. Get used to it. It's not going away."

He went to her couch and sank down onto it. "I'm embarrassed. And so damn tired. Why can I never sleep here?"

"Maybe you're afraid to relax and let some things just happen."

"You're right. Falling for you just happened." He chuckled and leaned his head back against the cushions. "And that's the best thing that's ever come out of coming home."

Willa's arms fell to her sides with surprise. "I keep telling you, stop dropping by when you're tired. You say things you shouldn't."

He lifted his head and looked at her seriously. "Why shouldn't I say that?"

"Because I'm not entirely sure you know who I am," she answered honestly. How could he, when she had only recently begun to figure it out?

"On the contrary. I've been paying very close attention."

She shook her head. "Tell me that in the morning, and I might believe you."

"Okay." He rubbed his hands on the couch on either side of him. "Can I sleep on your couch again? That was the only good night's sleep I've had since I've been here."

"Okay," she said, and sighed. "Let me get you a pillow."

"No, no pillow," he said as he stretched out, then made room for her. "Just you."

All sorts of things flew through her mind, the most surprising of which was the instantaneous *Yes!* she heard. But she'd been denying those instant impulses for far too long to follow them without some thought first. "Colin . . ."

"I just want you to lie here with me until I fall asleep, okay?"

She turned off the lights again, then walked over to him. He was so tall that she easily fit into his side. He put his arm around her, and she rested her head on his chest. This felt right.

What an impossible situation.

"I'm not sure I can live here," he said into the darkness, as if reading her thoughts. She could hear his voice deep in his chest.

"I'm not sure I can leave," she responded.

They were quiet for a while. His heartbeat was slowing to a calm rhythm.

"I think I might try to live here, though," he whispered.

"I think I might try to leave," she whispered back.

"But still no chance of turning you into a nature girl?"

She laughed and snuggled in deeper. "Go to sleep, Colin."

And, finally, he did.

❧

The next morning, Willa was standing on a chair in her closet, reaching back for a shoe box full of high school mementoes, when Colin said from behind her, "What are you doing?"

"That's funny, I was just wishing that a tall man would suddenly appear and help me," she said as she jumped off the chair. "Will you get that box off the shelf up there for me?"

He showed off by doing it easily.

"What is that?" Colin asked as he handed it to her.

"Just something I want to return to Paxton when I meet her today," she said as she set the box on her dresser. She'd been up for a while but wasn't dressed yet. Colin had still been asleep when she'd woken up, so she'd been trying not to make too much noise.

"So this is your room," he said, looking around. The wrought-iron bed was the one she'd slept in for most of her life, but the lamps on the bedside tables were funky crystal ones Rachel had given to her for her birthday. Her furniture was old, but some pieces were hand-painted with harlequin designs by one of her artist friends from National Street.

"Yes, this is my room."

He had a serious case of bed head, his shirt was untucked, and his feet were bare, which for some reason she found endearing. He turned to her and said, "I slept."

"I know." She wasn't going to tell him that she hadn't. She was used to sleeping on her back and, short of sprawling out on top of him, that had been impossible last night.

He walked up to her and put his arms around her waist. "Thank you."

"I didn't do anything."

"Yes, you did. And you know what this means?" He bent down and said into her ear, "It means we're going to have to do it again."

She laughed. "Okay, just not on the couch again. I'm too used to my bed."

FOURTEEN

Lost and Found

Just after lunch that Sunday, Paxton met Willa in the parking lot of the nursing home and they walked together to Nana Osgood's room. Willa was pensive but cheery, almost as though she was cautiously optimistic about something. Paxton wondered if it had anything to do with her brother not coming home last night. She really wanted to ask Willa but figured that was the kind of thing you shared only with friends.

"How are you with all that Nana Osgood told us on Friday?" Paxton said. "I couldn't ask you yesterday, not with Sebastian and Colin there."

"I'm okay. How are you?" Willa looked up at her, a line of concern forming between her brows.

"I'm okay, too," she lied. "A little worried about what more she has in store for us today, though."

"Well, it can't get worse, so that means it can only get better, right?"

"Right," Paxton said doubtfully, but she really did want to believe it. Something had to give.

Paxton had brought a box of chocolate truffles with her to give to Nana Osgood, even though her mother had said not to. But Paxton was tired of trying to be a buffer between Nana Osgood and her daughter-in-law, who fought like a snake and a mongoose. That was their battle, not hers. And she had enough to deal with.

Once Paxton gave Nana Osgood the chocolates, she settled beside her on the love seat. She did this gently, so she wouldn't dislodge her grandmother, who probably weighed as much as burnt paper. Willa sat in the chair opposite them.

Agatha stroked the box of chocolates on her lap. The first thing she said was, "If the police go after Georgie, I want you to tell them what I told you."

"I don't think they're going after her," Willa said. "I haven't heard anything from Woody Olsen. Have you?" Willa asked Paxton.

"No."

"I don't care what you think," Agatha said. "If it comes down to it, promise me you'll tell them!"

"It's all right, Nana. We promise."

"Okay, then." She petted the chocolate box some more.

"The gala is this Friday," Paxton said. "I still want you to come."

Agatha pshawed. "You silly girls."

"Willa and I noticed the date of the formation of the

Women's Society Club is around the same time Tucker
Devlin disappeared seventy-five years ago. Is that just a
coincidence?"

"No, it's not a coincidence. There's no such thing.
The night we buried him, I told Georgie I'd always be
there for her. She was afraid. She was pregnant. And I
was going to help her, no matter what. The next day I
got our four other best friends together and told them
Georgie needed us. I didn't give them the details, but
the town seemed to know Tucker was gone. Everything
felt different, like we were waking up. The six of us
formed the Women's Society Club exclusively to help
Georgie. We promised that we would never turn our
backs on each other again. Even if it made us afraid,
even if it was dangerous, we promised we would stick
together and make things right, because no one else
would. Georgie's family did nothing to help her. And
the whole town saw how Tucker treated us, pitting us
against each other, and did nothing to save their
daughters' hearts. We decided to become a society of
women, a club to make sure women were protected.
The club was something important back then. Not like
it is today."

"What happened to make it change so much?" Paxton asked. She'd been having mixed feelings about the
club lately, and finding this out just made her more
confused about her role in it.

"Life happened," Agatha said. "Georgie left the club
about ten years later, when the rest of us started having
our own children. That's when we began to use the
club as a way to compare notes. Who had the best

cook. Whose husband made more money. Georgie's life was so different that I don't think she felt like she belonged anymore. But I kept my promise. I was always there if she needed me. She just stopped asking. I was close enough to Ham, though, that he would come to me when she wouldn't."

"Grandmother Georgie was very strict with my father," Willa said. Paxton turned to her. She didn't understand the context, but Willa was obviously going somewhere with this.

"She was terrified he was going to turn out just like Tucker. She was terrified of everything. She was terrified this very thing was going to happen, that Tucker's body was going to be found." Agatha shook her head. "All her superstitions were because she wanted his ghost to stay buried. It turned into a mania."

"Did my dad know who his father was?"

"She eventually told him he was a traveling salesman she never saw again. I think he might have deduced more. What Ham knew for sure was that living a small life was what his mother wanted for him. And he did that for her. It was a shame he died just as he was finally coming into his own."

Willa leaned forward. "What do you mean?"

"He was going to sell his house and travel."

"He never told me that!"

"I don't think he told you a lot of things."

Willa surprised Paxton by asking, "Did he quit his job at the school because of me?"

"Yes. He was impressed by you. Although I can't

imagine why." Agatha made a face. "All those pranks. And when he found out you'd dropped out of college, he just thought you were finding yourself."

"He knew I dropped out?" It didn't seem possible, but Willa's brows rose even more.

"Of course he knew."

"How do *you* know?" Paxton asked, amazed that her grandmother had been harboring not only her own secrets but Willa's father's as well. What else was in that hard head of hers? All these years, Paxton had thought her grandmother was nothing more than a mean old lady. But she had a complexity and depth that no one suspected.

"Ham and I had a very long conversation when the time came for him to move his mother into a nursing home. He was going to travel. I promised I'd watch over Georgie." She straightened her shoulders. "Not that I ever stopped."

Willa sat back in her seat, seeming to think things over. Paxton used that opportunity to ask, "Why did you never tell me the club had lost its way? Maybe I could have done something."

"Paxton, I think you've tried to make the club more about the deed than the social aspect, and I give you credit for that, but I also believe it's more because you don't have friends than because of a higher calling." Paxton reared back at that. "Friendship started that club, and if you ever want to see it back to what it was, you have to understand what it means to be a friend. I know you've always looked at me and thought, *I don't want to be like her.* Well, here's your chance. People always say life is too short for regrets. But the truth is, it's too long."

"Will you come to the gala?" Paxton asked again. "I think it's important that you be there."

"Maybe. Keep bringing me chocolate like this and . . . maybe. Leave me to eat in peace," she said, opening the box.

Paxton and Willa stood, and each was lost in her own thoughts as they walked down the corridor. Paxton was heading toward the front doors when Willa stopped.

"I'm going to see my grandmother," Willa said.

"Oh. Right. Okay."

"Do you want to have some coffee first?" Willa pointed over her shoulder, toward the dining room.

Paxton smiled, almost relieved. "Yes. That would be nice."

They got their cups and filled them, and then they walked to a table near a window that overlooked the side garden.

"Why do you think we never became friends?" Paxton asked as Willa was emptying a packet of sugar into her coffee. "I've always been aware of the way you looked at me. You never liked me, did you?"

"It's not that," Willa said.

"What is it, then?"

Willa hesitated. "I guess it was jealousy in high school. I hated not having what you had. I ended up resenting my family because of it, and I wish I could take that back. As adults, I don't know." Willa shrugged.

"You set an impossible standard, and no one can live up to it. And sometimes it seems like you do it on purpose. Your clothes are perfect. Your hair is perfect. You juggle a work schedule that would take three normal people to manage. Not all of us can do that."

Paxton looked into her coffee cup. "Maybe I do do it on purpose. But it's only because everyone else seems happier than I am. They have their own homes, husbands, children, businesses. I sometimes think there's something wrong with me."

"There's nothing wrong with you," Willa said. "Why did *you* never make friends with *me*?"

"Oh, that's simple." Paxton smiled as she looked up. "You scared me." That made Willa laugh. "Seriously. You were so quiet and intense. Like you could see right through people. If I had known you were the Joker sooner, maybe it would have been easier to get to know you. I would have at least known you had a sense of humor. Then, when you came back, you didn't seem to want anything to do with the people you grew up with. You took up with the National Street set like you were thumbing your nose at us, like we were silly yokels."

"It's not that," Willa said immediately. "It's not that at all. After my dad died, I came back here to the realization that I could never say I was sorry for making it seem like he didn't do enough. I made a promise to myself, and to him, to be happy with what I had. Every day. But being around people I grew up with brought back all those insecurities at first, so I just got used to avoiding it."

"There's no avoiding me now, you know," she said. "You know my secrets. You maced people for me. You've got me for life."

Willa laughed and tried to wave that off. "Any of your friends would have done the same thing."

"No," Paxton said. "They wouldn't."

"Oh, I almost forgot," Willa said, reaching into the back pocket of her jeans. "I need to return this to you." She handed Paxton a folded piece of notebook paper.

"What is it?"

"It's a note you dropped one day in the hallway at school. I picked it up and read it. After that, I was just too embarrassed to return it to you."

Paxton took it and opened it. As soon as she realized what it was, she laughed in surprise. "My list of qualities in the man I wanted to marry."

"I'm sorry," Willa said sheepishly.

"This is how you forged my handwriting with that note to Robbie Roberts!"

"Yes. I'm really, really sorry."

Paxton shook her head and put the note in her tote bag. "That's okay. It's just a list. One of many. I'd completely forgotten about it."

"It's an impressive list," Willa said.

"I knew what I wanted back then." Paxton smiled and decided to go ahead and ask Willa what she was dying to know. "Speaking of wanting. My brother didn't come home last night. I don't suppose you know anything about that?"

Willa looked away. "He might have slept on my couch."

"Then why are you blushing?"

Willa turned back to her with a glint in her eye. "I might have slept there with him."

"I knew it!"

They laughed, and she suddenly felt like she was on such good footing with Willa. She never thought she was good at making friends. But maybe she was just trying to be friends with the wrong people.

They ended up talking long after their coffee had gone cold.

PAXTON OSGOOD'S FUTURE HUSBAND

Will be kind
Will be funny
Will be accepting
Will be able to cook
Will be a good kisser
Will smell good
Will always surprise me
Will argue with me and sometimes let me win,
    but not always
Will be mysterious
Will always love me, no matter what I look like
Mama will not like him, which means
    I will love him even more

Hours later, after they left the dining room and Willa went to see her grandmother, Paxton got in her car and immediately took the note out of her tote bag and read the list again.

She remembered losing it and panicking for days

about where it could be. She'd been afraid some ridiculous boy like Robbie Roberts would find it and tease
her. But years passed and she'd forgotten about it, one
of many things she'd managed to leave behind.

Where did this girl go? Paxton wondered. It was just
like looking at that old photo of her grandmother.
Where did this girl go? Colin said she was the only one
in their group who hadn't changed. But she had, and
not in a good way.

The girl she used to be would not approve of the
woman she'd become. That girl always assumed she'd
be happy at this age, as happy as she'd been back then.
What happened?

She sat there, staring into space, the note on her lap,
until her cellphone rang.

She looked at the screen. It was her mother, probably wondering why she wasn't home yet for the last fitting of her dress for the gala.

With a sigh, she put the phone and the note back in
her tote bag and started the car, then drove away.

Back to life as she knew it.

FIFTEEN

The Risk

Monday afternoon, Paxton worked through lunch in order to give herself the rest of the afternoon off. Paperwork requiring her signature was piling up at the outreach center, and there were a million little details to attend to before the gala on Friday night, but there were some things that were just more important.

She drove into the lot of Harris & Associates Realty, which was located next to the organic market, and parked her car. When she walked in, she saw Kirsty Lemon on the phone at her desk. As soon as she hung up, Paxton walked over to her.

"Paxton," Kirsty said, surprised. "What are you doing here?"

"I noticed that the townhouse on Teal Street is still on the market."

"Yes, it's still on the market," Kirsty said carefully.

"I want to buy it."

Kirsty looked cautious, distrustful, which Paxton wasn't expecting. "Are you sure this time?"

"Yes."

Kirsty sighed and grabbed her keys. "Well, let's go look at it," she said with all the enthusiasm of a person going in for a colonoscopy.

They both got in Kirsty's minivan. Paxton couldn't remember the last time they'd been in the same car together. It might have been as long ago as high school, when Kirsty would borrow her father's ancient Range Rover and they'd drive into Asheville on Saturdays. She missed that, being in the car with Kirsty, talking about everything. Before adulthood. Before there were so many things they didn't want each other to know.

The townhouse was in a community called Water-view, a pretty green place with a common that had a gazebo and a fountain. The homes were red-brick colonial and beautiful. The townhouse Paxton had loved from the moment Kirsty showed it to her last year was in a cul-de-sac. Wisteria vines grew around the door, and Paxton remembered thinking how wonderful it would be to walk in and out in the springtime, when the wisteria would be in full bloom. It would be like walking through a wedding arch every day.

Kirsty unlocked the security box. Inside were cathedral ceilings and hardwood floors. Upstairs were three bedrooms. That had been one of the points of contention with her mother when Paxton had wanted to move out last year, before she turned thirty. Her mother had insisted Paxton didn't need so much room.

She thought about what Sebastian said about every life needing a little space, and how that leaves room for good things to enter it.

She wished she had thought of that to say to her mother at the time.

Paxton walked around the open living space. The cook's kitchen off the living room was separated by a counter. She thought of how nice it would be to have friends over for dinner, idealizing things, of course, because the club members were married and that kind of girls' night out didn't seem to exist among them anymore. Or if it did, Paxton wasn't included. If she had done this right out of college, maybe things would have been different, before all their lives got so complicated.

"It's as beautiful as I remembered," Paxton said.

Kirsty was standing by the front door. "I was counting on the commission from the sale of this place last year. When you decided not to buy it at the last minute, I was so upset with you."

Startled, Paxton turned to her. "Why didn't you say anything?"

Kirsty shrugged.

"I'm sorry. We used to be able to tell each other anything. When did that change?"

"I don't know." Kirsty walked forward. "When you're a teenager, your friends are your life. When you grow up, friendships seem to get pushed further and further back, until it seems like a luxury, a frivolity, like a bubble bath."

"You're important to me, Kirsty," Paxton said. "You always have been. For some reason I just stopped saying it, showing it."

"Wow, Pax, this is a side of you I haven't seen in a while. What brought this on?"

"With the gala coming up, I've been thinking about our grandmothers, about how their friendships lasted their whole lives. I always thought it would be like that for us."

Kirsty looked a little sad. "Me, too."

And that was it, Paxton supposed. The acknowledgment that things had changed but that no one was willing to do anything about it.

"Okay. I want this place," Paxton said. "As quickly as possible. I'm making an offer today."

❧

"Paxton, come here," her mother called from the living room as soon as Paxton got in. When Paxton entered, her mother and father were sitting on the couch, watching the evening news.

"Your dress was brought back today," Sophia said, indicating the large white box on the corner chair. "Be sure to try it on in case there are some last-minute alterations. I think you and your daddy and I should all go together, particularly since you don't have a date."

Paxton walked over to the box and opened it, still feeling a little of that thrill she used to have at the thought of party dresses, the fantasy of it all. She smiled when she saw the shimmering pink material, the sparkling jewels at the neckline.

"I have to be there early, so I'm driving myself." She put the lid back on the box. "Mama, when did you move out of your parents' house?"

Sophia turned away from the television. "After college. I moved in with a few of my girlfriends. I was with them for about two years before I started dating your daddy. It was one of the best times of my life. When Donald asked me to marry him, I was thrilled, of course, but a little sad, too. It meant leaving my friends behind."

Paxton saw her father turn his head to look at Sophia when she said that.

"Why?" Paxton asked. "Couldn't you have still been friends?"

"Surely you know this, Paxton. You make a choice. You're not as close to your married friends as you once were, are you?"

"No," she said. "But I think that's like saying I'm sorry I left the water on and flooded the house. At some point, you could have turned it off. It's not like it had to happen."

Sophia suddenly frowned. "Why are you asking these things?"

Paxton picked up the dress box and walked over to her mother. "Because I'm moving out."

Sophia waved that away with a flick of her wrist. "Oh, Paxton, we went over this last year. You're much better off here. You don't need a place of your own when Hickory Cottage has so much room."

"I've waited too long. I've put it off too long. You moved out right after college. All my friends did, too. I need to do this." She took a deep breath. "I put in an offer on a townhouse this afternoon."

When it finally dawned on her that Paxton was serious, Sophia said, "Paxton! You didn't!"

"Yes, I did. You can come see me any time you want. And I'll visit you here. But I'm decorating how I want to decorate. And I'm not giving you a set of keys. I'm thirty years old, Mama. I think you've forgotten."

"Donald!" Sophia said. "Say something."

Her father turned to her, with a sparkle she hadn't seen in a while. "Would you like a down payment as a housewarming gift?"

That made Paxton smile. "No thanks, Daddy."

"Donald!"

"She's leaving, Sophia. Maybe it's time to try to work on just being you and me for a while."

As Paxton left, Sophia was looking at her husband as if he'd just come back from a very, very long trip—and she wasn't sure whether she was glad to see him or not.

When Paxton got to the pool house, she picked up the phone and called Willa. She wasn't even sure why.

"Hello?"

Paxton hesitated a moment. "Hi. It's Paxton."

"It's your sister," Willa said.

"Colin is there?"

"Yes. Do you want to talk to him?" Willa was in a good mood. Paxton could hear it in her voice.

"No, I want to talk to you. But I'll call back when you're not busy," Paxton rushed to say.

"Don't be silly." Paxton heard the squeak of a screen door, then the pop as it closed. "Now I'm outside," Willa said. "Your brother is trying to figure out my father's coffee percolator. He says it should be in a museum."

Paxton picked up the dress box she'd left on the couch and took it to her room. "He drinks too much caffeine."

"I know. I bought him decaf."

"I noticed today that you still haven't RSVPed for the gala. Will you come? Please? I won't make you accept something on your grandmother's behalf. I'd just like you to be there. And if Colin hasn't asked you yet, be prepared, he's about to." Paxton took the pink sheath dress out of the box and put it on a padded hanger, then hung it on the closet door. "I think I've even managed to convince Nana Osgood to come. After all she told us, I think she's coming just to see what a mockery this generation has made of the club."

"What's wrong, Pax?" Willa asked, and Paxton realized it was the first time she'd used the shortened version of her name. "You sound melancholy."

"Not melancholy. Conflicted, I guess." Paxton sat on the edge of the bed, looking at the dress. "I decided to buy a house today. I'm going to move out of Hickory Cottage."

"That's great! Do you need help moving?"

"Actually, I don't have much to move. I'm going to have to buy a lot of stuff. I don't even have a bed that's mine. I'm going to carve out some time to go take measurements tomorrow." She paused. "Do you want to come see the place?"

"I'd love to," Willa said immediately.

"Don't tell Colin yet. I'll tell him when he gets here. He's going to gloat." Paxton leaned forward, an elbow on her knee, her head in her hand. "I'm a little scared, Willa," she said softly, as though she was afraid to even say it.

She heard another creak, as if Willa had just sat down. "Happiness is a risk. If you're not a little scared, then you're not doing it right."

Paxton was silent, letting that sink in.

"Are you going to the gala with Sebastian?" Willa finally asked.

"He hasn't mentioned it. I think I'll be going alone. And that's okay. I'll be okay."

"Are you sure?"

"It doesn't feel the same with him. It doesn't feel the same without him. Nothing is really broke, so it's not like I can fix it. I just have to keep trying to find what I'm looking for."

"You'll find it," Willa said.

"I hope so."

"I'm here if you need me."

That, ultimately, was why she called. She needed to hear that. "Thanks, Willa."

SIXTEEN

Shedding the Armor

"Dr. Rogers will see you now," the receptionist said to Willa. "His private office is around the corner."

It had been a long shot, and Willa had waited almost an hour, but now she was finally going to talk to Sebastian. "Thank you," she said, entering the inner sanctum and trying not to look into rooms where the whirring and swishing noises were coming from. It made her queasy. She'd always hated dentists' offices.

She entered Sebastian's personal office, but he wasn't there. She took one of the two seats in front of his desk and looked around. It was nice but utilitarian. It didn't look as though he spent a lot of time here. There was only one photograph on his desk. When she turned the frame around, she saw it was a photograph of him and Paxton, one where they'd held the camera in front of them and grinned as they snapped the shot.

She heard Sebastian's voice in the hall and quickly turned the photo back around. Sebastian entered and smiled at her. He didn't have on his suit jacket, and his shirtsleeves were rolled up. He was so strangely beautiful. He hid it behind a lot of makeup in high school, but he seemed to have come to terms with it now. She was staring at him, but she realized he was probably used to it.

"You've done a nice job with the office," Willa finally said. "It doesn't look anything like I remember Dr. Kostovo's office."

He walked behind the desk and sat. "You mean it doesn't look like a medieval torture chamber anymore."

"Yes," she said, shuddering. "Who does that? In a dentist's office? As if half the patients aren't scared enough already."

"You should have seen his house when I first moved in," Sebastian said. "He left behind a suit of armor."

"You're kidding!"

"No. It's in my basement."

Willa laughed. "You should give it to Paxton as a housewarming gift. Can you imagine the look on her face?"

His brow knitted. "Housewarming gift?"

"She bought a townhouse." Willa paused, suddenly questioning her being there. In a fit of indignation, she had decided that if Sebastian didn't know how much grief he was causing Paxton, then someone had to tell him. But maybe this wasn't such a good idea, after all. "I take it she didn't tell you."

"No."

"Oh."

There was an awkward moment before Sebastian asked, "Is that why you came to see me?"

"Not exactly."

He nodded in understanding. "I always wondered why none of the other people in her life have confronted me. I think they assume she knows exactly what she's doing. To answer the first question I know you want to ask: Yes, I know Paxton is in love with me. To answer the second question: No, I don't want to hurt her. I've been doing everything in my power not to."

"Then try something else," Willa said as she stood. "It's not working." She reached over and took a notepad and pen from his desktop. She wrote something down and handed it to him.

"What is this?"

"Her new address. Her schedule is really tight, because the gala is in three days. But I happen to know she'll be there between four and five today."

He nodded as he stood, putting the note in his pocket.

Willa opened his office door and walked out, and Sebastian followed. He escorted her to the front desk, putting his hand on her back, low and firm. That's when she finally understood. Just like that. *I needed to stop being what everyone thought I was.* That's what he'd said outside her store on Saturday.

Startled, she turned to look at him, and he winked.

Oh, Paxton, she thought. *You have no idea what's in store for you.*

She walked out into the sunshine, smiling. Fate never promises to tell you everything up front. You aren't always shown the path in life you're supposed to take. But if there was one thing she'd learned in the past few weeks, it was that sometimes, when you're really lucky, you meet someone with a map.

Happiness meant taking risks. No one had ever told Paxton that before. It was like a secret the world had been keeping from her. Paxton didn't take risks, at least not when she was sober. She knew what she was getting into before she ever committed to anything. The fact that all the changes she'd made in the past few days scared her to death had to be a good sign.

At four o'clock, she let herself into the townhouse with the keys Kirsty Lemon had let her borrow. Willa had called her earlier, telling her she couldn't make it after all. So Paxton put the box of doughnuts she'd just bought on the kitchen counter and decided to use this time to do what she did best.

Make lists.

She was on the sixth sheet of paper when the doorbell rang. She was going from room to room, taking measurements and drawing little pictures of what she thought would go where. She took the earbuds of her iPod out of her ears and walked to the door, thinking maybe Willa was able to break away from work, after all. She checked her watch. It was a quarter till five. She was going to have to leave soon, but there was still time to give her a quick tour.

She opened the door, and the one person she wasn't expecting was the very person who stood there.

He'd loosened his tie, and his hair looked like he'd run his hands through it one too many times. "Sebastian," she said. "How did you know I was here?"

"Willa told me," he said. "Why didn't you?"

Willa told him? She stepped back numbly and let him enter. "It happened pretty quickly."

"This is a big step for you."

"It should have happened a long time ago."

He looked around, his hands in his pockets. He seemed so shut off that it made her heart ache. "I have a question," he said. "One I can't stop asking myself. Why did you kiss me when you'd seen me kiss another man all those years ago? Is there some twisted side to you I don't know about, Pax? Did it turn you on?"

She was caught off guard by the question. "No," she said, appalled. "It wasn't like that at all." He stared at her, and she shook her head. "God, Sebastian, people fall in love all the time. And it's not always with the right people. And it's not always reciprocated. I fell in love with you. I couldn't help it. I couldn't stop it. But I was prepared to deal with it in silence until it went away, or at least lessened to the point where I could see you and not want you so much. That night at the pool house, I was out of control, and I hated the feeling, and then you came by because you were worried about me when no one else was. If you cared that much about me, I thought maybe I could turn it into something more. It was careless and selfish and, as I have said time and time again, I'm sorry. I don't know what else to say."

"Sit down," he said. "I have something to tell you."

"I don't have any chairs. And I don't think I want to hear anything you have to say right now."

He walked over to her and took her arm. He led her to the stairs. "Sit down and listen to me," he said in a tone she wasn't familiar with. He was *nervous*.

She slowly sat. She set her notebook and iPod next to her on the step, then folded her hands in her lap.

He stood in front of her for a moment. Then he started pacing. "I didn't belong anywhere growing up," he finally said. "Not at home, not at school. As a teenager, I spent a lot of time at that diner on the highway, mostly as a way to keep from going home and facing my father. One Saturday night when I was sixteen, I was sitting there in the back booth, it was probably three in the morning, when a group of teenage boys came in, asking for directions back to Asheville. They'd gotten lost coming home from some party they'd gone to in South Carolina. They were loud, flamboyant, happy, not like anyone I'd ever met before. One of them spotted me, and it was like he'd spotted a lost member of his tribe. He came back to me and started flirting. His friends joined him, and we all had coffee and laughed. A door suddenly opened for me, this door of *acceptance*. Hours later, they said they had to go, that their mothers were going to be mad enough as it was. But they said if I could find a way to Asheville, they hung out at Pack Square every afternoon, and if I wanted to join them, I could. Then that boy who had first come over to me, Alex, ran his hand over my hair and said, 'Who knew something this beautiful grew way out in the backwoods?' " Sebastian shook his head. "I think humans are basically pack animals. And I finally found a pack. I'd never had one before."

"Are these the same boys I saw you with at the Asheville Mall?" Paxton asked.

"Yes. And the boy you saw kiss me was Alex. It was a confusing time for me. Those were my friends. They saved me. And on some level, I loved them. I loved Alex. But the reason I became one of them is that I needed to belong somewhere and they took me in. I didn't become one of them because I was one of them." He gave her a look she knew meant that what he'd said was significant, but she didn't understand.

"What does that mean?"

"It means I'm not gay, Pax," he said.

She felt his words burn into her skin.

"When I entered college, I started seeing a counselor who helped me work through some issues. The best, most accepting people I've ever known were gay. But it was a fallback position for me, and it wasn't who I was inside. So I began to date women in college, and I even fell in love a couple of times. But it never worked out because none of them understood me—they saw me as a platonic friend, or thought they were converting me. Those were some interesting years, and not ones I would ever care to repeat. It got to the point where I was simply tired of trying to defend myself. How people choose to live their lives, and who they fall in love with, should never *have* to be defended. So I made the decision about five years ago to not address my sexuality in any situation anymore. And that decision made life so much easier. Until I met you."

She stood. She wasn't going to cry. No matter how much she wanted to. "What kind of game are you playing with me? I don't deserve this from you, Sebastian."

She tried to walk past him, but he grabbed her by the arms and made her face him. "I'm not playing a game," he said in short, measured words, words that dropped like falling off a cliff.

"Then why are you telling me this?"

He let his hands drop. She swayed a little. "Because I love you in a way that's deep and raw and terrifying. And I don't know what to do. I've never felt anything like what I felt when you kissed me."

He was scared. She could see it so clearly now. "Then why did you stop it?"

He ran his hands through his hair. "Because I was still clinging to my conviction that sex only ever gets in the way of good relationships."

She swallowed. "And now?"

"My past will always be with me. It's a part of who I am. And I didn't think there was a single person in the world who could know everything about me and love me anyway. Until I met you. I love you, Paxton, and I have every intention of being with you forever, if you'll have me."

She'd been in his position just weeks ago. She knew what it felt like to stand in front of someone and ask them to love you, to try to pull them to you by the sheer force of your desire, a force so strong it felt as though you were going to die from it. She didn't stop to think. She knew only that she didn't want him to feel the way she'd felt. She reached for him and kissed him. Her arms wrapped around him, holding on for dear life. He backed her against the wall and her head thumped against it, but she didn't stop. She pushed at his jacket until it was off, then reached for his tie. Their hands were everywhere, getting in the way. Paxton lost her balance when the toe of her bare foot got caught in the cuff of his trousers, and she went down, taking him with her.

Sebastian rolled over, pinning her to the floor. She reached, trying to pull his lips down to hers again, but he resisted.

"I need you to say it," he said, breathless.

She looked up at him, confused. "Say what?"

"That you'll have me."

She suddenly thought about that list she'd made in high school. "You're everything I've ever wanted, Sebastian."

He kissed her again, and she worked at the buttons on his shirt. One of them popped off, and she heard it tick across the bare floor. "Are we going to do this here?" he asked against her lips. "We can go back to my place."

"No. Here. Now."

She felt his smile. "At least I know you don't love me for my furniture."

"Don't you dare bring over that suit of armor."

He lifted his head again. "Willa told you?"

Her hands went to his hair. "Some things she tells me, some things she leaves out." Like telling her Sebastian was coming over.

He lifted one brow. "So you compare notes?"

"Yes."

"Then I better make this good."

She hesitated. "It already is," she whispered.

❧

An hour later, Paxton woke up to her cellphone ringing. She reached over Sebastian to her tote bag but couldn't find the phone. She ended up dumping the contents out onto the carpet and fumbling through them until she found it.

She felt Sebastian put a hand on her back and lightly stroke.

She looked at the screen. It was Maria, the manager at the Madam. She'd had an appointment with her an hour ago about last-minute details with the gala. She groaned as she put the phone down and turned to Sebastian. "I have to go."

"Okay." He sat up and winced as he scooted back to lean against the wall.

"Are you all right?" Paxton got up and started picking her clothes up off the floor.

"My back. This is why I don't camp out. Can I buy you a bed as a housewarming gift?"

She smiled as she dressed, well aware of the fact that he was watching. It didn't bother her, for probably the first time in her life. "I've seen your bed," she said. "You have very good taste in beds."

"You could try it out, you know. To get a feel for it."

She walked over to him and went to her knees beside him. "This is real, isn't it? It really happened."

He put his hand to her hair. "Regrets?"

She took a deep breath. All she smelled was cut grass from the open living room window and the sugary smell of the doughnuts she'd brought in and put on the counter. "None," she said. "What about you?"

"Not a single one. Well, maybe the lack of bed. Love me, love my creature comforts."

She took his hand in hers. "I do love you, Sebastian. And I'm scared out of my mind."

"That makes two of us."

"Willa said happiness means taking risks. And if you're not a little scared, you're not doing it right."

That made him laugh. "If that's the case, we have nothing to worry about," he said, leaning forward to kiss her. "Let's be terrified together again."

Which ended up making Paxton another hour late.

SEVENTEEN

Fly Away

Wednesday morning, Willa got to her store before Rachel did, so she started taking the chairs off the café tables by the large window, which was as blank as a movie screen because of the morning mist. Occasionally, the lights from a car would speed by, and it was unquestionably a local. Only locals knew where they were going at this time of morning. Tourists got lost and drove slowly in circles until the fog lifted.

She had just started the coffee when the bell above the door rang and Paxton entered.

"Hi," Willa said, surprised. "What are you doing here?"

Paxton shrugged. "I was taking a different way to work this morning and saw your light."

"Would you like some coffee?"

"Yes, that would be great. Extra cream, no sugar," Paxton said.

Willa flipped through Rachel's coffee notebook on the bar and said, "According to my barista, Rachel, your coffee order means you want comfort but you're afraid to ask for it."

Paxton didn't ask who Rachel was, or what strange coffee anthropology she was studying. She just laughed and said, "That is uncomfortably accurate."

"She claims it's a science."

"This is a great store," Paxton said, looking around. There was a short silence before she finally said, "Actually, I stopped by to thank you."

"For what?" Willa asked as she poured the coffee into two large red-and-white-striped cups.

"For going to see Sebastian yesterday. For telling him to come see me."

Willa picked up the two coffee cups and walked to a café table. "So, things worked out?"

"They worked out very well," Paxton said as they pulled out chairs and sat. "I actually stayed at his place last night."

That made Willa grin. "*That's* why you were taking a different way to work this morning."

Paxton hid her smile behind her cup of coffee. "Guilty. I take it Colin stayed with you?"

"I left him asleep. I didn't have the heart to wake him up."

"My mother is probably having a conniption right now," Paxton said.

"You don't sound too unhappy about that."

"I'm not."

Willa leaned back in her seat. "So what's on your agenda today?"

"I'll be at the Madam all day. Last-minute details for the gala. Plus, I have to write my speech." Paxton gave her a worried look. "You're still coming, aren't you?"

"Yes. I'm going to wear that vintage beaded dress your grandmother gave Georgie."

Paxton gasped. "Oh, Willa, that's *perfect*."

The bell over the door rang, and they both turned in their seats. Woody Olsen had just entered.

As always, it took Willa a moment to recover when she saw him, to see past all the potential bad news he could bring.

Paxton said, "Good morning, Detective Olsen."

Willa finally found her voice. "Woody, what are you doing here?"

He stood awkwardly by the door. "I'm on my way to work. I saw your light. I worried you by coming in here a couple of weeks ago, and I wanted to put your mind at ease. Maybe it's good that you're here, too, Paxton. I was going to tell you today. We can't determine the cause of death of that skeleton found at the Madam. There was trauma to the skull, but it also appeared that he'd suffered what would have been a fatal fall. Maybe it was an accident. I don't think we'll ever know what happened, or how he got there."

"A *fall*?" Paxton repeated.

"Excuse me a moment," Willa said to Paxton as she stood and walked over to Woody. "I've been thinking about when you were in here last. You asked me if I recognized anything in that suitcase buried with the skeleton. You were talking about the photo in the scrapbook, weren't you? The photo of Tucker Devlin that looks so much like my dad."

Except for his eyes darting once to Paxton, who was still at the table and deep in thought, Woody gave nothing away in his expression. "I was the only one who made the connection. And I didn't say a thing."

"Thanks, Woody."

He nodded. "Your dad was a wonderful man. Best teacher I ever had."

The bell over the door rang again. Woody automatically stepped out of the way to let whoever it was enter. But no one was there.

"Don't pay any attention to that," Willa said. "It's been doing it a lot. I think it's broken."

"You know that old superstition, don't you, the one that says when you hear a bell ring, good fortune is pouring down? It means you should cup your hands out and catch it."

Willa automatically held her hands out. "Like this?"

"Exactly," he said as he turned to leave. "Now I bet your bell is fixed."

Willa smiled and shook her head, then she walked back to Paxton. "I think what he was really trying to tell me was that my grandmother was in the clear. So now we know Agatha won't be dragged into this, either."

"But I don't get it," Paxton said. "If Tucker Devlin died from a fall, why did Nana Osgood say she killed him?"

Willa wrapped her hands around her warm coffee

cup. "I have a feeling our grandmothers never wanted anyone to know the whole story."

"But what could be worse than what Nana Osgood told us?"

Willa raised her brows. "Do you really want to know?"

"No, you're right," Paxton said, shaking her head. "It's time for things to finally be laid to rest."

&

When Paxton drove to the Madam two hours before the gala was to begin on Friday night, the sky was twilight blue and the windows in the Madam were bright yellow against the evening clouds, giving the impression that the sun had actually set into the house itself and was now sitting inside. The old oak tree by the house was steadied by several cables tethered to the ground, and spotlights were aimed at it. The effect was like an old performer onstage, basking in the glow of one last ovation. As she approached, she could see the leaves on the tree shaking slightly, which was partly from the sprinkler system in the branches to keep it hydrated while it took root, but also from the dozens of birds that had flown here en masse and had taken up residence in the tree. They'd been the bane of Colin's existence all week. He could get them to fly away, but they always came back.

She parked and walked up the front steps, her breath catching in her chest. The restoration was finally complete, and it was beautiful. This house stood as a testimony to life, to friendship, to good things coming out of bad situations. And she had no idea it would mean this much when work first started on the place.

Once she was inside, she did a walk-through. The interior was lovely in the evening, the lighting designed to cast a warm yellow glow off the dark paneling in every room. The banquet hall was decorated with sparkly streamers and lighted floral arrangements on every table. Every place setting had a small book documenting the charities the club had supported over the years, including some essays by past recipients of the scholarships they'd given out, as well as gift bags containing custom candles and chocolates, all with the seventy-fifth anniversary logo on them. At the dais in front of the room was a lectern and a large screen, on which flashed photographs of club members throughout the years. There was a string quartet in the corner, tuning up.

Later, when she was in the kitchen, checking to see if everything was on schedule, she heard the music cue up, then the murmur of voices out in the lobby. The first guests were arriving. Soon there were people mingling everywhere, and waiters were carrying trays of champagne and hors d'oeuvres that seemed to float through the crowd. Paxton greeted everyone, including her mother and father, who, despite all the time and work that went into this place, had never actually seen it since that first day, over a year ago, when they'd toured the property and decided to make it an Osgood venture to restore it.

Her father was impressed, but her mother admitted nothing. She still wasn't happy about Paxton moving

out, and was even less happy when Paxton started referring to Sebastian as her boyfriend. But Paxton loved
her mother and accepted her as she was. She even took
it in stride when her mother found out she was seated
with Nana Osgood and demanded her place card be
moved to another table. Nana Osgood had arrived earlier with the nurse Paxton had hired to attend to her
that night, and was the only one seated in the banquet
hall. Paxton wondered what Nana Osgood thought
about being here, after all these years. But when she'd
first arrived, all she'd done was complain about the
heat and demand a cocktail.

The last-minute seating change was the first in a few
minor emergencies that took Paxton away until the
food was ready to be served. She had just straightened
out a room switch upstairs and was about to walk down
to tell Maria to cue everyone to be seated when she
stopped at the top of the staircase and looked down.

It was a dreamlike setting of princess gowns and
black ties. It was magical, everything she'd hoped it
would be. But she was ready for it to be over, because
the gala had been planned around everything that the
Women's Society Club shouldn't be. And she'd fallen
right into the trap.

With some relief, she saw that Willa and Colin had
finally arrived. Willa looked beautiful, like something
out of time in that vintage dress, and for a moment Paxton could almost see Willa's grandmother as a young
woman, sweeping through the rooms here at the
Madam. Colin stood close to her. Paxton knew her
brother well enough to recognize the subtle shift that

was happening in him. She'd seen him often at the
Madam that week as the landscaping was being com-
pleted, and he'd seemed centered, almost calm. He'd
once even asked her if there were any other town-
houses near hers up for sale. He'd like to have a home
base for when he came back for visits, he'd said, with a
subtext that was so obvious it was almost too good to be
true. She was careful not to make too much of it, but it
still made her heart soar. Sebastian, Willa, and now
Colin. Sebastian had been right. If you make room in
your life, good things will enter.

Paxton caught the manager's eye and nodded, and
the signal was given that everyone should now enter
the banquet hall.

Paxton went to the ladies' room and checked her
makeup, then stared at herself, telling herself that she
really could go through with this.

Sebastian had waited for her at the back of the banquet hall once everyone had been seated. She hadn't
seen him in two days, and she'd felt it physically, like a
withdrawal. They'd called each other often, but it
wasn't the same. She wanted to touch him, to have him
near. It was still so new. She was afraid of losing it. But
gala preparations had kept her at the Madam until the
early hours of the morning for the past few days. Last
night, she'd even slept here, and had only gone back to
Hickory Cottage to change.

"You look lovely, darling," Sebastian said when she
entered.

"I'm so glad you're here." She took his hands and
squeezed them. He had to feel that she was trembling.

"Everything is perfect. I was surprised to see you even managed to get your grandmother to come. How much did it take to get one of the nurses to escort Agatha tonight?"

A smile twitched at her lips. "You don't want to know."

"It's almost over." He leaned in and said, "I've missed you."

She let that wash over her, warm and comforting. "I've missed you, too."

"I know you haven't had time to order furniture for your house," he said.

"I've been too busy. It's next on my list."

"I had a bed delivered there today," Sebastian said.

That made her laugh. "Are you kidding?"

"No."

"Then I can't wait to go home," she said.

"I can't wait to take you there. I have some very good memories in that house already." He led her to the dais at the front of the room, then whispered, "Good luck. You'll do great." The quartet ended their tune. There was applause as she walked to the lectern, and Paxton watched as Sebastian took a seat at the table with Willa and Colin and Nana Osgood.

Her insides were shaking, and she thought for a moment that she couldn't go through with this. But then she thought of her grandmother and Georgie, how everything about this house and the club had to do with them, with honoring them, and she knew it was the right decision.

She cleared her throat and said, "Welcome, everyone, to the Walls of Water Women's Society Club seventy-fifth anniversary gala."

More applause.

"I wrote a speech months ago. Those who know me aren't surprised. I'm such a planner." Some people laughed. "The speech was about what good work we've done and how proud we should be of ourselves." She paused. "But I tore it up this week, because I realized we've gotten it all wrong."

There was a change in the air. Everyone seemed to realize something was up.

"This club was formed to help each other. Not others. *Each other.* As in, we're all in this together. It wasn't formed to set us apart from others, or to compete with one another. It was formed because seventy-five years ago, two best friends in the darkest moments of their lives said, *All we have is our deep and abiding love for each other. We can't lose that or we lose ourselves. If we don't help each other, who will?* I don't know when it happened, and I don't know how, but the Women's Society Club lost its true focus. It's not what it was, and I can't bring it back. That's why I'm stepping down as president tonight, and removing my name from the roster." The room started to rumble. "I have not always been the best friend to any of you," she continued, searching the crowd for Kirsty Lemon, for Moira Kinley, for Stacy Herbst and Honor Redford. "But I can promise that from this night forward, I will be there for you if you need me, anytime, anyplace. That's the true nature of the club. It was never meant to be an institution. It was a pinkie swear among teenagers who were afraid, and knowing that they could count on each other made them feel better. Our grandmothers knew they would be friends for their entire lives. How many of us can say that? How can we know the true meaning of charity if we don't even know how to help those closest to us?" Paxton stepped back. "That's all I wanted to say."

She rubbed her forehead, squinting against the spotlight. The room was silent. Suddenly, everyone turned toward a small sound coming from a table in front.

Agatha was chuckling, the sound rusty, like a piece of machinery that hadn't been used in years. "That's my girl," she said.

&

There wasn't much celebrating to be done after that. Dinner was served, then awards were given out and some more speeches were made, but the ceremony had a hurried and awkward feel to it, and most were eager to leave. It would go down as a small disaster and a definite scandal, but it gave people something to talk about, which made them happy. Paxton didn't care. It was the right thing to do, and she felt so much better now, even if her mother wasn't talking to her.

Most people avoided Paxton as they left. She was sure everyone wanted to talk to one another about it first, to come to some consensus about how they all felt about it. One way or the other, Paxton knew that those who decided to stick with her would be her true friends. The others would just be scenery.

At the end of the evening, Paxton and Willa walked Agatha out to the nurse's car, after Agatha had given them a blind tour of the Madam, pointing out by feel and memory everything she remembered about the house. She and Georgie sliding down the banister and their skirts flying up. Playing dolls in Georgie's room. Having pineapple upside-down cake the Jacksons' cook would make in a cast-iron frying pan, so that the brown sugar on top turned crispy. A slide-away secret compartment in the bookcase where they used to leave notes for each other.

"I'm proud of you, Paxton. This place smells new. Different. It's a good place again," Agatha said, wobbling slightly as Willa and Paxton helped her down the front steps. Paxton wasn't sure, but her grandmother might have been a little drunk. "And what you did in there tonight, that took guts."

"Thank you, Nana. Mama may never speak to me again."

"Her loss." Before Agatha got in the nurse's car, she said, "You and Willa, I think you might have finally made him go away. Real friendship was the only thing he was afraid of."

"Him?" Willa asked.

"Tucker. He's been around these past few weeks. Haven't you noticed? I've felt him. There's been a strange sweet scent in the air. And you can't tell me you haven't seen birds acting strangely lately."

Willa and Paxton moved in closer to each other as Agatha got in the car and the nurse reached over and buckled her seat belt. "What really happened here, Nana? Did you really . . ." Paxton couldn't finish the sentence, not with the nurse there.

"Yes, I did," Agatha said. "Don't forget."

Paxton and Willa watched the car drive off, then gave each other odd looks. Just as they turned to walk back up the steps, the scent of peaches permeated the air for a moment, thick and cloying, before it faded into the night, crossing the moon in a wisp of smoke, then disappearing. Suddenly, the oak tree began to shake as dozens of birds took flight, their dark wings showing flashes of yellow like fireworks.

"Coincidence?" Willa asked, wrapping her arm in Paxton's.

"There's no such thing," Paxton answered, holding on tight as they watched the birds fly away.

EIGHTEEN

The Peach Keepers

1936

The first time it happened, Georgie woke up, suddenly freezing. She didn't know why. It was so hot that summer that she had to sleep on top of her bedsheets, and she still melted every night. But that night she woke up to her perspiration freezing and cracking on her skin. She shivered and looked to the window, expecting to see the world frozen over. The world was changing, she thought sleepily. It had been changing for months. And now that Tucker, with his charming smile and magical ways, had moved into the Madam with them, Georgie felt the changes even more. There was a lot of hope in the air, hope that their financial problems would soon be over with this peach orchard they were planning. And her father, who ignored her on good days and blamed her for her mother's death during childbirth on bad ones, even seemed happy to see her at dinner now. He was happy to see her because Tucker was happy to see her. Tucker changed people that way. And because of that she ignored the way he would brush up against her in the hallways, how he was always around when she got out of the bath. She ignored his restlessness and the way his temper would flare up sometimes. Agatha had told her she was being silly, anyway, and that she had no idea how lucky she was. Tucker had changed Agatha, too. She'd once been able to tell Agatha anything, but now Agatha burned with something hot every time she saw Georgie, and Georgie didn't know why. Georgie had felt very alone lately. She didn't realize just how alone she was up here on Jackson Hill until her friends stopped coming to see her. And at parties, they ignored her. So Georgie spent most of her time in her room now, mending dresses so she could wear them one more year, or rearranging the dolls displayed in her cupboard, brushing their hair and ironing their aprons, and dreaming of the day when all these changes would be over and they could all go back to being normal again.

There was the smell of smoke and peaches around her that night as she sat up, shivering in her bed. She was used to that, the peach smell, anyway. Tucker carried it on his skin. It followed him around wherever he went. That's why he said birds bothered him so— because they liked the way he smelled. Georgie had never argued, but she'd always thought the birds swooping down on him seemed angry, not enamored.

She looked around her dark room, and that's when

she saw a small orange light by the door. The lit end of
a cigarette. *Someone was standing by her closed door.*
Her heart leapt in her chest. It felt like a fist striking
her from inside.

Tucker walked out of the shadow. He put the cigarette to his lips and took a puff, brightening his face
and making it glow. He dropped the cigarette to the
floor and stepped on it, and everything was dark again.

When he came to her, she didn't understand what
was happening. When he finally left, she stayed in her
bed for the rest of the night, too afraid to get up. She
heard him come back down from his attic bedroom in
the morning, pause by her door, then walk away. When
the house was quiet, she finally got up and washed, but
then she propped a chair against the doorknob and
wouldn't let anyone in until her father demanded she
join them for dinner. A week, two weeks, passed, and
Tucker made no move toward her again, and she
thought that was it. She'd actually begun to recover.
Her world was no longer the same, but she knew she
would survive.

But then he came back.

It went on all summer. No matter how many times
she reached out for help, no one listened to her. He
made them not listen. She couldn't see an end to it. It
was going to go on like this forever unless she stopped
it. But she wasn't that brave. She'd never been that
brave.

Until the day she finally accepted that she was pregnant.

That day, she took the cook's frying pan to her room

with her. And when night fell, she stood behind her door and waited.

After she hit him, an odd thud that sounded like something being dropped in the next room, she just stood there, as if waiting for everything to go back to the way it was. She began to tremble. Nothing was different. She was still pregnant. And she had just hurt Tucker, maybe even killed him. Her father would never understand. No one would understand. Except . . .

"Show him to me," Agatha said after Georgie had run to her house in the mist, tripping and falling along the way so that when she finally got to Hickory Cottage she was covered with dirt and scratches. She knew the way into the house that led to the back stairs, the stairs they'd used to sneak past Agatha's parents many times. She'd woken Agatha up and begged her to listen, begged her to help. She trusted Agatha more than anyone in the world. And what had happened this summer couldn't possibly have erased a lifetime of friendship. It didn't just go away like that. At least, she prayed it didn't. She'd lost so much already.

Agatha was strangely quiet as Georgie led her back up to the Madam. Tucker was right where she had left him, on the floor of her bedroom. The frying pan was sitting on his chest, like a weight keeping him from floating away. Agatha knelt by him, muttering something Georgie couldn't understand. She put one of her hands on his head, then jerked back as if she'd been burned. She stood and said, "We have to do this quick. He's not all gone. And he's angry. We have to dig a hole close by. We can't carry him far. It has to be in the yard here. If we do it on the hill, it'll wash. Hurry, Georgie, let's get started." This was what Agatha was so good at, taking charge, organizing, breaking things down into manageable bits.

They worked by candlelight. In the kitchen, Georgie sifted together pepper and sawdust the carpenter bees had created when they'd burrowed into the porch. The cook had once told her that if you sprinkle sawdust and pepper in front of a door, no one would be able to leave that room. She put it in front of the doors to her father's and brother's bedrooms, hoping it would give her and Agatha time to do what they needed to do.

They dug in the yard for hours, as far away from the house as they could but not so close to the precipice that the hill would give way. She would never forget how quiet it was. The mist below them hid the town from sight but also muffled everything. It felt as though they were the only people in the world, two young women about to bury the symbol of their helplessness, as if that's all it would take to make them whole again.

The half-moon had fled across the night sky by the time Agatha said the hole was big enough.

They had to go back into the Madam to get him. They dragged him to the window in Georgie's room and pushed him out. Then they took him by his arms and legs and half carried, half dragged him across the backyard, leaving a trail of black as though lightning had scorched the earth.

After they were done, they stood there as the sun rose over the mist. They were dirty and shaky and mostly numb.

Agatha finally turned to Georgie and embraced her. It took a moment for Georgie to realize that Agatha was crying, and Agatha never cried.

"Oh, Agatha," Georgie said. "I'm so sorry."

"No!" Agatha said, pulling back. "You have nothing to be sorry about. This is my fault. What kind of friend lets this happen? I'm sorry. I'm so very sorry."

"What am I going to do?" Georgie asked. "Tell me what to do, Agatha."

"We'll get through this. Don't worry. No matter what happens, I'm here for you. I'll never let you down again."

"What if they find out it was me?"

Agatha took her hand. "As long as I'm alive, Georgie, no one will ever know it was you. I promise."

And seventy-five years later, Agatha had kept that promise.

arms and held her head against his chest. Paxton stopped in front of Sebastian. He handed her his drink, then put one hand around her waist, pulling her to him and kissing her.

The four of them went back to the banquet hall, saying goodbye to the last of the guests, the ones staying there that night, and they took a seat at one of the tables. They ended up staying all night, talking and laughing, while the cleanup crew worked around them.

This was the first time Willa had seen Paxton and Sebastian act like a couple, confidently and unabashedly. Watching them, she realized they made so much sense together. Every look, every touch, was a reassurance, almost electric, as if they were shocking each other with every contact.

As for her and Colin, they were acting as though they were taking it a day at a time, having fun and not taking things too seriously, but that was all it was, an act. They were far more serious than either one was prepared to admit. They had been talking a lot lately about what they wanted to do. Was Colin really ready to move back? Was Willa ready to leave? Knowing that her father had had plans to leave, even with his mother in the nursing home, made it a less complicated question than it had once been. They had decided that Willa would come with him back to New York for a few weeks, then he would come back with her to Walls of Water for another few weeks, and then stretch it out longer and longer until they both knew what was right. They hadn't told anyone yet. They were still at that stage where they were asking each other if they were really going to go through with it. But really, the moment it first came up, they had both made up their minds. They each wanted to be where the other was, and it didn't matter where.

The future was theirs to take.

When daylight came, Paxton and Willa were still awake, their stocking feet propped in the men's laps, but Colin and Sebastian had their heads on their table. Colin had a silver streamer draped over his shoulders and a flower from the centerpiece behind his ear. Willa had decorated him while he'd slept. He was snoring slightly.

Paxton looked to Willa, and Willa laughed quietly. "I'll still take him," she whispered.

Paxton took her feet out of Sebastian's lap and stood. "I'm going to see about getting some breakfast brought out. I'm hungry. Are you?"

"Starving. Should I wake them?" Willa asked.

"Not yet." Paxton turned to walk away, then stopped. "Willa?"

"Yes?"

"I'm glad you came tonight. I'm glad . . . " She didn't seem to know how to finish the sentence. But Willa understood.

"I maced people for you," Willa said. "You've got me for life."

When Paxton left, Willa closed her eyes. If the future was hers to take, then she tried to imagine what it was going to be like.

She imagined that from that day on, whenever she and Paxton would meet unexpectedly on the sidewalk, or in a store, they would laugh, like sharing a secret only they knew. Grandmother Georgie would still be here, because it was impossible to think of a future without her. Willa knew that one day she would be gone, but for now, in this future she was creating, Georgie was hanging on. Agatha would continue to look after her, and they would all make sure Agatha had all the chocolates she wanted. Willa and Colin would divide their time between New York and Walls of Water for a few years, leaving Rachel to manage the store and further her coffee studies. Rachel would probably publish a book about it one day, and would coin the term *coffeeology.* Willa and Colin would come home for good when Willa got pregnant. *Pregnant.* It was a far-off thought, but it still gave her a crazy feeling in her stomach, like planning the biggest and best adventure. Sebastian and Paxton, on the other hand, would probably get married right away and have three children in quick succession. They were kinetic that way. Throughout marriages and children, Willa and Paxton would still call each other almost every night, sometimes just to say good night. Sometimes Willa would know it was Paxton without her ever having to say a word. She would be in bed, Colin asleep beside her, and the phone would ring and she would pick it up and say, "Good night, Paxton. I'm here if you need me."

That, they knew, was true friendship.

And they knew, if you're lucky enough to find it, you hold on to it.

Hold on, and never let it go.

She opened her eyes and saw that Colin had woken

up. His hair was tousled, and his eyes were still droopy with sleep. He smiled at her, rubbing his hands along her legs. He looked punch-drunk and happy as he said, "I just had the most amazing dream."

She smiled back and said, "Me, too."

ACKNOWLEDGMENTS

A bushel and a peck to Andrea Cirillo and Shauna Summers. Thank you for your support and guidance. Love to my family for putting up with me while I was writing this book, when I was often more pit than peach. And a big thanks to Daphne Atkeson for helping me see this from bud to blossom.

ABOUT THE AUTHOR

SARAH ADDISON ALLEN was born and raised in Asheville, North Carolina, where she is currently at work on her next novel.

ABOUT THE TYPE

This book was set in Fairfield, the first typeface from the hand of the distinguished American artist and engraver Rudolph Ruzicka (1883–1978). Ruzicka was born in Bohemia and came to America in 1894. He set up his own shop, devoted to wood engraving and printing, in New York in 1913 after a varied career working as a wood engraver, in photoengraving and banknote printing plants, and as an art director and freelance artist. He designed and illustrated many books, and was the creator of a considerable list of individual prints—wood engraving, line engravings on copper, and aquatints.